Forever Yours (Maybe)

One wrong turn. No way out.
And the last place she expected to fall in love.

Also by Kathryn Kaleigh

The Gravity of Us Series

(Reading Order)

Just Breathe

Just Surface

Just Melt

Standalone Suspense

Out of Ashes

CONTEMPORARY

Alpine Falls (Maybe Yours) Series

(Reading Order)

Still Yours (Maybe)

Yours for Christmas (Maybe)

Forever Yours (Maybe)

(ALPINE FALLS)

Stranded in Alpine Falls

Belonging in Alpine Falls

The Spirit of Christmas in Alpine Falls

Christmas Wishes in Alpine Falls

Finding True North in Alpine Falls

A Ghost of Christmas Magic in Alpine Falls

Secrets and Second Chances

Honeymoon with a Stranger

Not Our Wedding

(SILVER PINES)

The Way Back to You

Back to Where We Began

When We Were Us

(ONCE UPON FOREVER)

My Forever Guy

Our Forever Love

Forever Vows

Finding Forever

Accidentally Forever

(TRUE NORTH)

Borrowed Until Monday

Still Mine

The Moon and the Stars at Christmas

Perfectly Mismatched

On the Way to Forever

A Merry Little Christmas

On the Way Home to Christmas

It was Always You

(UNBREAK MY HEART)

Begin Again

Love Again

Falling Again

(FOR THE LOVE OF THE FLIGHT)

Just Stay

Just Chance

Just Believe

Just Us

Just Once

Just Happened

Just Maybe

Just Pretend

Just Because

(MAGNETIC NORTH)

Second Chance Kisses

Second Chance Secrets

First Time Charm

Three Broken Rules

Second Chance Destiny

Unexpected Vows

(FALLING FOR CHRISTMAS)

The Heart of Christmas

The Magic of Christmas

In a One Horse Open Sleigh

A Secret Royal Christmas

An Old Fashioned Christmas

(CITY SKYLINE BILLIONAIRES)

Billionaire's Unexpected Landing

Billionaire's Accidental Girlfriend

Billionaire's Fallen Angel

Billionaire's Secret Crush

Billionaire's Barefoot Bride

(TRULY, MADLY, DEEPLY)

The Lady in the Red Dress

On the Edge of Chance

Sealed with a Kiss

Kiss Me at Midnight

The Heart Knows

(STOLEN ECHOES)

When Cupid's Arrow Strikes

Chasing Fireflies

A Chance Encounter

(EDGE OF THE HORIZON)

The Forever Equation

Pretend Boyfriend

All our Tomorrows

Kissing for Keeps

Out of the Blue

The Princess and the Playboy

(RED LIPSTICK KISSES)

Red Lipstick Kisses and Small Town Wishes

Stolen Dances and Big City Chances

Chance Connections and Upside Down Plans

A Christmas Kiss on the Twenty-Fifth

Believe in the Magic of Christmas

Vows of Inheritance Series

(Reading Order)

Vow to Protect

Vow to Redeem

ROMANTASY

(IN THE SPIRIT OF LOVE)

Spirits of the Heart

Out of Dreams and Ashes

Etched Upon the Heart

WESTERN ROMANCE

(LONE STAR HEARTS)

Wanted by a Texas Ranger

Saved by a Texas Ranger

(WHISKEY SPRINGS)

Finding Natalie

Promising Samantha

Falling for Allyson

Saving Savannah

Claiming Charlie

Rescuing Keira

Protecting Gabriella

Courting Isabella

TIME TRAVEL

(INTO THE MIST)

Written in the Wind

Scripted in the Stars

Destined in the Twilight

Promised in the Mist

Trapped in the Melody

(DRAGON'S BLOOD)

Dragon's Blood

Lavender Blue

Champagne Silver

Twilight Frost

Mountbatten Pink

(WHEN HEARTSTRINGS BECKON)

Rescued in Time

Meet me in 1879

(WHEN HEARTSTRINGS ECHO)

Messages Across Time

Falling Through to Forever

Once Upon a Winter's Spell

(BECKONED)

Before the Storm

Twist of Fate

When the Stars Align

Once Upon a Christmas

Once in a Blue Moon

A Wish Upon a Star

(BEGUILED)

When Lightning Strikes

Storm of Time

Midnight Storm

When the Moon Falls

Stormborn Angel

(SPELLED)

Time Tempest

The Heart Remembers

A Moment in Time

Moonlight Shadows

HISTORICAL

(TAPESTRY OF BLUE AND GRAY)

Shadows Beneath Magnolia Blooms

Secrets Among Southern Roses

(IT HAPPENED BY ACCIDENT)

Accidentally Alluring

Accidentally Married

(SOUTHERN BELLE CIVIL WAR)

Beyond Enemy Lines

Love Always

Hearts Under Siege

Hearts Under Fire

Away Down South in Dixie

The Reluctant Bride

Stay with Me

Jasmine Kisses

Magnolia Kisses

Gardenia Kisses

(THE QUINNS)

Wait for Me

Take Me Home

Keep Me Safe

FATED MATES

Riley's Mate

Aiden's Mate

Brayden's Mate

STANDALONE SUSPENSE

Lost and Found

All I Want for Christmas

Serenity

Courting Alley Cat

Forever Yours (Maybe)

THE ALPINE FALLS (MAYBE YOURS) SERIES

KATHRYN KALEIGH

Forever Yours (Maybe)

Chapter One

Madison Lane

It seemed like a good idea at the time.

That's my life. Or so it seems at this juncture in my twenty-seven years.

It seemed like a good idea to take a road trip, by myself, instead of flying to my friend's wedding. When I'd studied the map, the drive hadn't looked all that bad. Just get on Interstate 10 and head west from Houston, then north on Interstate 25 to Denver and east on Interstate 70 to Alpine Falls.

Simple enough.

It was simple enough until I got out of the car in El Paso and my cell phone fell out face down onto the concrete parking lot, smashing the screen, making it impossible for me even unlock it.

Unfortunately, of course, I lost all my phone numbers. It was quite a shock to realize that I don't have a single phone number other than my own memorized.

I don't even have my friend Hannah's address. All I know is it is somewhere in Alpine Falls, Colorado. So that's what I put in my GPS and hope for the best.

After that the trip is uneventful until I leave Denver and head into the mountains.

It's two days before Christmas Eve, Hannah's wedding date, and the weather is appropriately cloudy and gloomy for December. The forecast is calling for snow.

I don't have a lot of experience with mountain life, but I'm determined to make it to Alpine Falls before it starts snowing.

I take the designated exit off of Interstate 70 and head north along a curvy two-lane highway. It's picturesque. I have to give it that. Mountaintops covered with caps of snow. Wispy clouds hovering below the tops of those jagged mountains.

The road follows alongside a rushing mountain stream with shallow, sparkling clear water tumbling over a rocky riverbed. And there are trees everywhere. Blue spruce trees on either side of the highway mixed with white-barked aspen trees and maple trees, both of which lost their leaves months ago.

I drive past a little cabin with smoke wafting out of the chimney sending a wave of nostalgia washing over me. I imagine a family gathered around the cozy fireplace, watching a movie or reading or just talking. The scent of fresh baked cookies fills the air. Or maybe an apple pie.

It's Christmastime and that's what families do. But not my family. My parents decided that since my brother left home, they would take advantage of the long anticipated freedom and take a cruise somewhere warm.

My brother is in Atlanta spending Christmas with his girlfriend.

And that's basically how I ended up here. Driving along a lonely country road in the mountains. Blindly following my GPS to a little town called Alpine Falls.

I could have (probably should have) stopped somewhere to get my phone replaced, but I didn't want to waste the half a day I knew it would take.

Being late for my friend's wedding is not an option. It's already taking longer to get there than I planned. Being my first road trip and all, I might have underestimated the time it takes to drive halfway across the country.

"Turn right on Birch Road in five hundred feet." The female voice of my GPS says with no uncertainty.

"Seriously?" I confess to keeping up a conversation with my GPS since losing my cell phone. Not that it ever responds.

Since I'm at the mercy of my GPS and it's gotten me this far, I slow down and leave the highway to turn right onto Birch Road. Birch Road, a blacktopped country road, winds its way further up into the mountains. Definitely increasing in elevation.

My GPS then suggests I stop for food. Not a bad idea. Except that I don't see any signs of a town up ahead. In fact, I cross an area with a steep drop off on one side.

Beautiful, but deadly. That's what I call it.

After about a mile, I round a little curve and that's when I see the road sign. "Luchara. Elevation 8,540."

Not the population. The elevation. It's interesting how these little towns seem prouder of their elevation than they are of how many people live here.

But there's a little diner. The sign out front identifies it as "Luchara Diner." Not a very creative name, but it looks like it only attracts locals. There aren't enough cars on the highway to suggest that it's much of a tourist stop.

Well, why not? My GPS brought me here, so I might as well stop. I have to go to the bathroom anyway.

I turn down the gravel road and park next to the only other vehicle near the restaurant. The town's only street is a gravel road with parking on either side. There are only a few other parked cars scattered here and there along what I guess they would call Main Street.

The restaurant is the only building labeled with a sign. The other buildings are unidentified shops of one kind or another.

The restaurant has outdoor seating in the form of picnic tables, but it's too cold for anyone to be seated outside. The outside seating area looks quite inviting. A wooden deck with a live, very tall and old oak tree right in the middle of it, a circled bench around the perimeter of its trunk.

A little bell jingles over the door as I step inside and a man calls out to me from behind the kitchen.

"Have a seat wherever you like," he calls out in a gruff smoker's voice. The man is wearing a white apron and apparently is both the cook and the host.

Only two of the six tables are filled. A couple of bearded men in flannel shirts are seated at one of those tables. An older couple, obviously tourists from the way they're dressed are seated at the other one. He's wearing slacks and a polo shirt. She's wearing a casual dress and sandals.

I take a seat next to the door and pick up the sheet of paper that serves as a menu. Not a lot of variety. Everything has eggs in one form or another.

The man comes to stand next to me.

"That's the breakfast menu," he says, looking over my shoulder. "You can order from it if you want to, but this here is the lunch menu." He hands me another piece of paper with items that sound a lot more like lunch items. Hamburgers. French fries. A fried chicken plate.

"Can I get a hamburger? Well done?" I ask.

"Sure thing. Anything to drink?"

I hold up a bottle of water I brought in with me. "I'm good."

"Suit yourself. Got bottles of beer if you change your mind."

"I'll keep that in mind."

The cook/server leaves me alone at the table and heads back behind the counter to the kitchen.

The men laugh loudly at something one of them said.

I tap my fingers on the table. Without a cell phone, I have pretty much nothing to do to entertain myself.

I'm certain my friend Hannah and Olivia have tried to reach me by now. Hannah will be concerned that I'm not answering my phone, but Olivia, whom I've known since grade school, will think I'm just in one of my work mode periods.

I do that sometimes. I close myself off in my apartment and don't want to talk to anyone.

I might be introverted. But it's the only way I know to get everything done.

Right now I'm trying to start a business and it's not going like it's supposed to.

I literally have my life planned out on a spreadsheet. I'm twenty-five now and I'm supposed to have gotten my business off the ground by now.

It might be time for a pivot.

Fortunately, I have contingencies built into my spreadsheet.

It's definitely time to rearrange some things.

My hamburger and fries arrive. Finally. One thing I've discovered is that eating at restaurants alone without a cell phone is not fun. There's not only not anyone to talk to, but there's nothing to read or watch.

My first order of business after I make it to Alpine Falls is to get my cell phone replaced. I just have to get there first. To let them know I'm okay and that I'm not going to miss the wedding.

The wedding is a long story, but it's important to Hannah.

She's marrying her high school sweetheart Jack Thompson.

The funny thing about it is she spent the last ten years thinking she and Jack were divorced when in fact, they've been married all this time.

So technically Jack is already her husband, not her fiancé.

But since Hannah dated other guys and was actually engaged to someone else when she learned that she was still married to Jack, they feel like they should have a wedding to reset their marriage.

Personally, I think it's a good idea.

The hamburger isn't bad. I eat half of it and all my fries before going up to the counter to pay. Now that I've eaten, I'm ready to get going. I should be in Alpine Falls by the end of the day if my GPS is correct and I'm ready.

I'm wishing I could just fly home after the wedding, but, of course, I have my car.

Again. It seemed like a good idea at the time.

Chapter Two

Lucas Thompson

I LOCK the door to the cabin and walk the distance to the Luchara Diner. It only takes me fifteen minutes to get there, door to door. My big gangly black lab, Scout, runs along at my heels.

The old log cabin built in the last century is perfectly located for someone who cherishes privacy. A writer maybe. Or a retired couple. Maybe an investor who wants to rent it out in the summers.

So many possibilities.

The air has a definite bite to it and I shrug deeper into my fleece-lined coat. My boots crunch on frosty snow protected from the day's sunlight. The trail winds among a variety of trees, most of them, aspens and maples, with bare winter branches. Others, blue spruce trees mostly, have full branches that smell like Christmas.

I automatically glance at my watch. Two days before Christmas Eve. Two days before my brother's wedding. Tomorrow I need to pack up and make the short drive back to Alpine Falls.

I have little doubt that they've been trying to reach me, but since there's no cell phone service in Luchara, I wouldn't know.

Fortunately, since I have a habit of disappearing for weeks at the time, they don't expect much out of me. I established that habit during my party days. I never would have predicted that bad habit established in my college years would serve me well in the future. This time I have a legitimate reason for being off by myself.

As I near the diner, a police car pulls up and parks between two tourist's cars.

Luchara doesn't get very many visits by the police, certainly not state troopers. Either something happened or the policeman is just passing through. Luchara is a quiet little community. Another thing that makes it attractive.

That and it's just half an hour's drive from Alpine Falls.

The bell rings as I go inside the diner.

Mel is standing behind the counter, hands on his hips. The state police officer drags off his sun glasses and says something I can't hear.

There's a young lady standing at the counter, credit card in hand, waiting to pay.

The only other people in the diner are two loggers working in the area and an older touristy couple. Everyone is quietly watching the interaction between Mel and the policeman.

I walk up and lean an elbow on the counter. It has the desired effect. Both men look at me. Scout sits down behind me, but no one notices him.

"Everything okay?" I ask with my disarming expression that makes it hard for most people to admonish me for interrupting.

"No," Mel says in his gruff smoker's voice. He doesn't smoke anymore, but the gruffness stuck even after he quit. "There was an avalanche on Birch Road."

My gut twists. Birch Road is the only way to get from here back to the highway. I'm honestly surprised I didn't hear the avalanche. Was probably running the power saw when it happened.

"Anybody hurt?" I ask.

"Don't think so," the policeman says. "But the road is going to be blocked indefinitely."

"Wait," the young lady jumps in. I immediately detect a distinct southern drawl. She has the same accent as Olivia, a friend of my brother's fiancé/wife. Not from here. "I have to get to Alpine Falls."

"Not going to happen," the policeman says with nothing more than a halfway glance in her direction. "The road was washed off the side of the mountain."

She's shaking her head, but the policeman is talking to

Mel again. "Make a list of supplies you're going to need. I'll make sure they get helicoptered in."

"How are you getting out?" I ask the policeman.

"I'm not. No one is getting out." He looks at Mel again. "I hope you have a room for these people."

"The loggers have a trailer," Mel says. He nods in the direction of the older couple. "They're staying at the B&B. No other guests."

I look at the woman waiting to pay for her food. She crosses her arms.

She looks like a vexed elfin princess. Delicate features. Long brunette hair pulled back loosely, leaving a few strands framing her face.

Long dark eyelashes and the greenest eyes I've ever seen. Green like a lush verdant forest after a rain.

"I don't know where you're going to sleep," Mel says to the policeman, ignoring her.

"Hoping you have an extra room."

Mel sighs. "We'll figure something out."

"What about her?" The policeman asks, finally acknowledging the young lady's presence.

Everyone is looking at the young lady now.

"I can't stay here," she says, with a stubborn lift of her chin.

"Lady," the policeman says. "Unless you're planning on hiking out of here, which I don't recommend with the snow coming, you're not going anywhere."

"She can stay in my cabin," I say, blurting out the words

before I have time to think about just how impossible that will be.

Chapter Three

Madison

"I GUESS EVERYTHING IS SETTLED THEN," Mel, the cook and apparently the owner of this diner, says.

"I don't think so," I say, sliding my credit card into my coat pocket. Right now I have more important things to worry about than paying for a ten dollar meal.

Mel turns back to the stove and flips a burger while the policeman turns and walks outside, murmuring something into his radio.

With nothing left to do but to address the man who just offered me his cabin in the midst of this unfortunate event, I turn to face him.

He looks like he hasn't shaved in a couple of days, but

beneath that stubble is a handsome man. A breathtakingly handsome man with steel blue eyes pinned on mine.

"I can't stay in your cabin," I say.

"Suit yourself," he says with a little shrug.

"I have to get to Alpine Falls."

"Don't we all?" he says, signaling Mel. Mel throws together a hamburger, scoops up some fries, and slides the plate over to the man. He follows that up with a cold bottle of beer.

The man takes the plate and the beer to the nearest table and sits down to eat.

I'm at a loss. Stranded.

"Aren't there any rooms here?" I ask Mel. "There has to be someplace I can stay."

"Sorry ma'am. We have two rooms in town and they're both taken."

"What about your place?"

"Oh no," Mel says with a glance toward the policeman standing outside. "I've already got one unwanted guest in my one bedroom house. My wife is already going to kill me."

"Well," I say, looking over at the man who offered his cabin. "I don't know that man."

"Name's Lucas. I reckon he doesn't know you either."

Mel makes a good point. I glance over my shoulder at Lucas. He seems to have forgotten about me.

"I need to pay for my food," I say, sounding as weary as I feel.

Mel sends me a look that I interpret as him really not wanting to be bothered with ringing up my burger. Like everyone else, he suddenly has far more important things to think about.

If the avalanche washed out the road and snow is on the way, it could be spring before we have a way out of here.

I need to sit down.

I just drove over that road. Birch Road.

The avalanche could have so easily have happened as I was driving up here.

"Ten dollars even," Mel says.

I don't question him. Maybe there are no taxes here. Not seeing any place to scan my card, I hand it over to him. He places it on a little machine and manually makes an imprint of it. Then hands me a piece of paper to sign. I haven't seen one of these since I was a kid.

I sign it and hand it back.

"Is there some place in town where I can buy a cell phone?"

"A cell phone?" He scoffs. "We don't even have cell phone service here. Why would anyone try to sell a cell phone?"

"Has this ever happened before?" I ask him. "An avalanche?"

"Lady," he says. "As much as I'd like to stop and chat." He obviously does not want to chat with me. "I don't have the time. If you have any sense at all, you'll go over and introduce yourself to Lucas. He's your best bet right now and unless you want to take up sleeping in your car, you'll make nice with him."

I walk over to where Lucas is finishing up his burger and fries and drinking his beer.

"Hi," I say. "I'm Madison."

"I'm Lucas," he says, his expression blank, wiping his hands on a napkin.

"You said you have a cabin I can rent until we can get out of here?"

"The offer stands," he says, pushing his plate away.

"I didn't mean to offend you. I was just..." Looking away, I tuck a strand of hair behind an ear. Asking for favors is not one of my strengths. But he did offer. "Well. I was caught off guard."

"We're all a little caught off guard right now."

"Has this ever happened before?" I ask. "Just wondering how long we're going to be stuck here."

"It happens in the mountains. But it hasn't happened here. It could be a year before they have a road open again. Depends on the engineers."

My jaw drops along with my stomach. "A year?" I drop into the seat across from him. "Surely not."

"I'll walk down there tomorrow and take a look."

"Can I go?"

"Do you have hiking boots?"

"No."

"Then it's not a good idea." He pulls a treat out of his pocket and hands it to his dog. The dog sets it down at his feet and looks at me with big brown eyes.

"You have a dog," I say as though I just now noticed. "In a restaurant."

Lucas hesitates a moment as though he can't quite decide if he's supposed to provide an explanation. Finally he simply says. "His name is Scout."

"Scout." I slide out of my chair and kneel in front of the dog, holding out a hand for him to sniff. "Hi Scout. I'm Madison."

The dog licks my hand, then stands up and wags his tail, letting me pet him.

At least I've found one positive thing in the little community of Lachara. A friendly black lab.

As for what I'm going to do about being stranded here is another matter entirely.

No way out of here. My trusty GPS sent me into an impossible situation.

No cell phone and I don't have phone numbers to call my friends.

No place to stay unless I stay in Lucas's cabin.

Chapter Four

Lucas

WHILE SCARFING down my burger and fries, my thoughts are racing.

The avalanche changes everything, especially if it's as bad as the state trooper suggested. It's bad enough that the officer isn't able to get out, so there's that. I'll hike down at some point and take a look for myself, but I'm not optimistic.

The timing is the worst. I'd been planning on leaving here tomorrow. I should have left today, but that's tricky because leaving today, I could have been caught in the avalanche.

I'm so close to getting the outside of the cabin finished. If I don't get it finished before the snow settles in, it'll be spring. So I might as well resign myself to going ahead and moving to the inside renovations. This sets me back a bit, but not a lot and...

"Hi." I look up to find the young lady I'd seen standing at the counter now standing at my table. "I'm Madison," she says with a tentative smile.

"Lucas," I say.

I'm not from the south, but my mother, having grown up in the south, drilled being a gentleman into my head. My brothers and I all got a steady dose of how to treat a lady.

There's no way I could just leave a damsel in distress standing there. On the flip side, I'm not going to force my help onto someone who doesn't want it. I blame our independent mother for that one, too.

In the heat of the moment, as a gentleman, I'd offered for her to stay in my cabin. I'm quite familiar with Luchara and there really isn't anywhere else for her to crash.

Luchara is a small town community with a population of 65. There's not even a sheriff.

It's not a tourist town. Just a little community of people who live thirty minutes from Alpine Falls. There are all of two rentable rooms and they're obviously occupied at the moment.

And now we're all stranded for God knows how long.

My cabin is in no way whatsoever set up to have someone staying there. There's not even a bed. I'm sleeping on the floor in what can only be described as a construction zone.

But I do have heat and running water and electricity. So there is that.

Now that I've made the offer, I can't very well go back on it.

Besides, Scout obviously approves. In fact, he's making a fool of himself over her.

"I hope you don't mind dog germs," I say, thinking about my brother, Trenton, who likes dogs well enough as long as they don't lick his face.

"I'm friendly with them," Madison says, looking up at me with a happy grin on her face. "I don't have anywhere else to go," she says. "So thank you for letting me stay in your cabin."

"You might change your mind when you see it," I say. "I should warn you it's under construction."

"From what I'm told, it's my only option."

"Okay then," I say. "Did you already eat?"

"Yes. I was just about to leave."

"Good. The cabin doesn't have any food or a stove."

"Sounds like my kind of place."

I look at her sideways and wonder if maybe she misunderstood me. I decide to let it go. When she sees the cabin, she may decide that sleeping in her car isn't such a bad option after all.

Luchara does have a little gas pump hidden behind what passes for a General Store so if she decide to do something crazy like that, she'd at least have plenty of fuel.

"We should get you settled in then," I say.

"Okay." She stands up and secures her scarf around her neck. "I'm parked just outside."

"We walked," I say. "It's not far, so just follow us."

"Do you want to ride?" she asks.

"No. We'll walk. Scout has a propensity to shed and lick car windows."

"I don't mind dog hairs," she says.

"It's seriously not far," I say.

She shrugs. "Okay."

The little bell rings overhead as we step outside. It feels like it's dropped twenty degrees since I walked into the diner.

I hold onto Scout's collar and watch as she gets into her car.

We start walking ahead as she backs out.

I can't help but wonder what I've gone and done.

The cabin is so far from ready to have anyone other than me seeing it, much less staying in it.

I'm going to need to cut some firewood to make sure it's warm. And I'm going to need to come back and buy some more blankets and a pillow while she settles in.

The cabin is tucked deep in the trees sitting on the edge of the river. At night, the sounds of the river drift through the windows like a lullaby—one of the things that initially attracted me to the cabin.

Two sets of sawhorses are out front, a stack of lumber near them. Another stack of logs that I'm using to give the outside wall a refresh isn't far away.

While I wait for Madison to park her car, I pick up the

power saw I left outside when I went to lunch and stash it in metal storage crate in the back of my truck.

"This is it," I say as she gets out of her car. "I warned you. It's a work in progress."

"I don't mind. It's in a beautiful location," she says, closing her door. "The river sounds like a water fountain."

"Makes for good sleeping," I say. "Want help with your luggage?"

"Sure," she says. "I have an overnight bag in the back seat."

"Computer?" I ask.

"Didn't bring one," she says. "I don't have a laptop."

"Sometimes it's nice to take a break from technology."

"Sometimes that just happens," she says. "whether you want it to or not."

As I toss her overnight bag over my shoulder, Scout runs excited circles around her.

"He's just a puppy," she says, smiling.

"Yeah. Not sure how old he is. He was a stray."

"Aw. That makes me appreciate him—and you—even more."

Those little words of praise have me puffing out my chest with pride. I like it that I did something that pleases this girl.

I push open the door and let her walk in first.

"I feel like I should apologize for the state of the cabin, but it has heat and running water and electricity."

"No need to apologize," she says, stepping over a two by four lying in the floor.

"I need to pick up these hazards. Wasn't expecting company."

She walks to the bedroom door. Peeks inside.

The she turns around and faces me. "I don't see a bed," she says.

"There's no bed. But I'll light a fire and you can sleep on the floor. It'll be cozy."

"Cozy is good."

"I'm just going to put your bag over here on this counter."

"Thank you so much," she says.

"Don't mention it. I'll let you get settled in. I'm just going out to chop some firewood."

"Okay. Do you live nearby?"

"Not exactly," I say. "I'm stranded here. Like you."

She tilts her head and looks at me. "What do you mean?"

"I'm staying here, too. In the cabin."

Chapter Five

Madison

I STAND at the window and watch Lucas chopping firewood.

The cabin is warm inside. Heated by an electric heater and will be heated by the fireplace shortly.

There's no bed. Just a little stack of blankets, neatly folded in one corner. I give him points for the neatly folded blankets and equate it to a made up bed.

But there's no bed.

No kitchen. No problem. The diner is within walking distance and I don't eat all that much anyway.

There's a bedroom. But the bedroom doesn't have a fireplace. Or a heater.

According to Lucas, he's living here while he renovates the house. Not unusual.

Just a bit inconvenient considering that I'm going to be staying here with him—a perfect stranger.

Since Mel at the diner sort of, halfway, recommended I stay with Lucas, I suppose he's not a bad guy. Someone I can trust. It's not like a have a whole lot of choice.

Besides he has a sweet, loving dog. Only a good man could have a sweet, loving dog.

I turn away from the window and survey the cabin.

It could use some picking up.

I find a box of trash bags on the counter and gather up things that are obviously throw away. Like takeout coffee cups and food wrappers left lying around. I make a stack for things I'm not sure about. Like little chunks of wood. Lucas could have plans for those.

A few minutes later, Lucas comes inside, a load of firewood in his arms.

"You cleaned up," he says. "It looks better."

"I just picked up a few things," I say, inordinately pleased that he noticed and approved.

He stacks the firewood near the fireplace, then proceeds to lay logs in the hearth.

"Can you grab that newspaper over there?" he asks.

"Sure." I kneel next to him and crumple up pieces of newspaper for him to stuff in between the logs.

He pulls out a lighter and before long the fire is giving off a nice bit of heat.

"Do you need anything?" he asks. "I'm going to walk into town and buy some extra blankets."

"I don't think so. But I wouldn't mind going with you."

He takes a deep breath. "I need to bank the fire before we go."

"You just built it."

"It's okay. I can build it again."

"No. I didn't think about the fire. I'll just stay here."

But he's already putting out the fire. "Easy enough to build again when we get back. You might see something in town that you need."

"You're very kind," I say.

After he washes the soot off his hands, we put on our coats on and head back out into the cold.

Maybe staying here in front of the warm fireplace would have been a good idea after all. I don't know what I could possibly need from one of the little stores.

Scout runs ahead, circles through the trees, and comes galloping back up behind us.

"The cold weather agrees with him," I say, shoving my hands in my coat pockets, looking for warmth. My little wool coat is southern weight. Hannah had assured me that they have plenty of coats and I shouldn't worry about bringing anything heavy to wear.

Unfortunately I'd taken her at her word. Unfortunate because it looks like I'm going to miss the wedding.

A haze of wood smoke lingers over the town. All the buildings, it seems, have wood burning fireplaces.

"Is this all of Luchara?" I ask as Main Street comes into view.

"This is it."

"How far is it from Alpine Falls?"

"Twenty minutes or so. It's just a little community of people who wanted to be away from town."

"It sort of gives the term small town a new meaning."

"Yeah. I guess it does. It's super secluded for those who like that sort of thing."

"Do you? Like it? Or are you just working here on the cabin?"

"I don't mind it," he says, not really answering the question. Leaving me with even more questions than I had to begin with.

We walk past the diner, deserted now that it's the middle of the afternoon, and walk along a wooden sidewalk to one of the stores.

As Lucas opens the door and we all three, Scout included, step inside, a little bell overhead jingles, and an older man comes out of the back.

"Hello Lucas," he says. "I guess you came in to stock up on avalanche supplies."

"Hey Roosevelt. Guess you could say that. At least you have a good attitude about the whole thing."

"What else am I going to do? Not like I can change it."

"You working with Mel on putting together a list of supplies?"

"Sure. Mel called over here. I'm about to head over there so we can put our lists together."

"I won't keep you," Lucas say. "We just need some blankets and whatever Madison needs."

"I'll look around," I say.

The little store is tidy and has a variety of things from laundry detergent to bags of snack to postcards on the counter.

Apparently, even though it only has two rooms for rent, there's some touristy traffic.

Since I'm not sure how quickly the little town vendors are going to run out of supplies, I grab a big bag of chips and a tube of toothpaste.

I hesitate at the candle section. The cabin has heat, but we could always lose electricity. I grab a candle and tuck it in the crook of my arm.

Not seeing anything else I need, I rejoin Lucas at the front of the store. He's already got a stack of blankets and a pillow on the counter. A box of canned dog food. And a flashlight.

Seems he and I were thinking alike.

Roosevelt must be in the back again.

"I don't know if you noticed," he says. "but there's no cell phone service in Luchara. Do you need to use the phone? To let anyone know where you are?"

I shove my hands in my coat pockets and make a wry expression. "I hadn't noticed because my cell phone is broken. And yes. There are people I need to call, but their numbers are forever lost in my phone."

"Oh," he says, studying me. I can't help but wonder

what he's thinking. If this were one of those bad movies, he'd be thinking how if he killed me, no one would know.

"You said you're headed to Alpine Falls?"

"That's right."

"Hey Roosevelt." Roosevelt comes back out carrying a bag of dog food. "You got an Alpine Falls phone book?"

I look over at Lucas. I could almost kiss him. He's a genius.

"I had one. Haven't seen it since someone borrowed it. I'll look for it, though."

"Thanks. I'll check back with you."

"You need help carrying all this to your cabin?" Roosevelt asks.

Lucas glances at me. "Nah. I think we've got it." I nod in agreement.

"I'll put it on your tab."

"Thanks, man. And remember to look for that phone book."

"I'll ask Mel if he has one lying around someplace."

Lucas and I load up everything. He throws the bag of dog food over his shoulder. I take my lighter bag of chips and toothpaste and my candle. He takes the rest.

"Thanks for thinking of the phone book," I say. "I'd forgotten that they still make those."

"I've had to use one out here a couple of times. They're older. Probably at least ten years old, but unless someone is new to town, they should be in there."

Hannah and Jack grew up in Alpine Falls, but Hannah's parents don't live there anymore.

Now all I have to do is remember Jack's last name.

Chapter Six

Lucas

It doesn't take me long to get a nice cozy fire going again.

Madison arranges blankets and a pillow in front of it and sits down to read one of my science fiction novels I'd left lying around.

"Let me know if you need me to do anything," she says.

"I will," I say. "I just need to think through some plans for the bedroom."

"You're going to make some changes?" she asks, sitting up, her legs crossed Indian style and setting the book aside. "What kind of changes?"

I pull out a sketchpad and pencil and open it up to one of my previous drawings with precise measurements. I'm not an architect, but my brother is and I might have picked up a few things from him.

With Madison here, I've changed my perspective on some of my previous ideas.

"First of all," I say, studying the drawing. "I'm thinking to add a fireplace to the bedroom."

"That's a great idea." She gets up and walks into the bedroom.

"It should go right here," she says, correctly assuming I followed her to the door. She points to the outside wall between two windows. "It's the logical place. You won't disturb the load-bearing walls and there's still plenty of room for the bed on the other wall. With the windows on either side, add a couple of comfortable chairs and you've got a reading nook."

"Makes perfect sense," I say, wondering why I didn't think about just walking in here and looking around instead of trying to use the drawing to figure it out.

"What else?" she asks, but doesn't give me time to answer. "A free-standing bathtub. You could expand the bathroom and put the tub in front of a window overlooking the river. Do they make glass that's one way?"

"I'll check on that. I'm not sure I have time to add another room though. At least not right now." And since I'm planning on selling the cabin as soon as possible, probably never.

"That's okay. There's enough room in the bathroom for one if you take out one of the sinks and just have one."

"You don't like dual sinks?"

"I think a bathtub wins."

I run a hand over my chin. "It's good to get a female perspective."

"Happy to help."

"Where did you learn so much about design?"

We walk back into the living room and she sits back down on her little makeshift bed.

"It's just a hobby. I hope to make enough money someday that I can build my own house and when I do, I'll know exactly what I want. What about you? Are you an architect or a contractor?"

"Just a handyman," I say.

She nods towards the drawing I have open. "I think maybe you're selling yourself short."

"Maybe," I say. "But it's a just a hobby." I grin at her.

The truth is, since I don't have a degree in architecture, no one has ever taken my design work seriously. I've always been seen as the youngest son who parties and never held a real job. I was the football player who didn't make it to the pros.

But this cabin, if I can make it work, is my chance to save our family's ranch and prove that I can do something besides play sports.

No one had to tell me that the ranch is struggling financially. It's obvious. They laid off all the staff. Sold a few horses. The signs are all there.

After my father's accident, my oldest brother came home to run the ranch and he's doing all he can do. Now that he's getting married, his fiancé (wife) helps out, but it's still not enough. The income just doesn't outweigh the expenses. He has his own small jet and is able to help out by offering flights, but the truth is, they need a windfall.

If I have anything to do with it, I'm the windfall.

Missing my brother's wedding, though, is going to put me back in the doghouse. A doghouse I'm not sure I'll ever be able to climb out of. Even if this avalanche is out of my control.

I sketch in the ideas that Madison gave me. She is so right on target. Sometimes it just takes a fresh perspective.

"I'm going to take Scout out for a walk," I say.

"Okay," she says, not glancing up.

"Come on, Scout. Let's go out." Scout doesn't hesitate to get up and rush to the door.

I put on my coat and open the door. "Hey Madison," I say. "Come see."

Madison gets up and comes to the door.

Her whole face lights up. "It's snowing," she says, stepping outside. No coat.

She stands in the snow and turns her face up to it, her hair soon adorned with snowflakes.

Scout, equally delighted, rushes around trying to catch snowflakes with his mouth.

Crossing my arms, I stand there and watch them. My puppy trying to catch snowflakes and Madison, a southern girl delighted with falling snow.

It's almost worth missing my brother's wedding for.

I'll give her about two minutes before I'm going back inside for her coat.

Chapter Seven

Madison

THE FALLING SNOW, fat fluffy flakes fluttering from the sky, is delightful. I've seen flurries a couple of times. Houston is not without its winter moments. They're just few and far between.

But this snow, falling among the undecorated blue spruce trees is different. As I stand there with the first few flakes falling onto my face, the snow starts falling like silent rain.

Scout, who had been chasing snowflakes, trying to catch them with his mouth, sits down and barks.

I guess he decided if he couldn't catch the snow, he'd bark at it.

Lucas is standing at the cabin doorway watching us both with amusement.

"I'll get your coat," he says.

"It's okay," I say. "I think I'll go inside now."

"Good idea."

But instead of going inside, I stand beneath the alcove next to him while he waits for Scout to decide if it's safe to do his business.

"It's his first winter," I say.

"I think you're right."

"The snow makes it all seem like Christmas."

"It is Christmas."

"But doesn't it make you want to have hot cocoa and sit in front of the fireplace?"

"I guess so."

"You need a Christmas tree," I decide.

He looks over at me sideways.

"If we're going to be stuck here for Christmas, we should have a tree."

"I haven't decided that we're going to be stuck here," he says.

"But the avalanche."

"I'm going to hike down there tomorrow and take a look. See if we can walk out. Both of us need to get to Alpine Falls." He glances down at my sneakers.

"I know," I say. "I need hiking boots."

"Wouldn't hurt. But I don't think anyone in Luchara is going to have any you can buy."

"That's unfortunate," I say. "But these aren't bad."

"They'll be ruined if this snow keeps up."

"It'll be worth it. But... I do have a suitcase full of clothes I need to take with me."

"That might be a problem."

I sag against the door. "How do these things happen?"

"I don't know," he says. "From where I'm sitting, things could be a whole lot worse."

I smile to myself. Same. Things could be a whole lot worse.

Yes. It looks like I'm going to miss my friend's wedding. And yes. I broke my cell phone and now I can't get in touch with her.

And I'm stranded here in the middle of nowhere for who knows how long.

But. On the plus side, I'm stranded in the middle of nowhere with a handsome man who's interesting and has a super cool dog.

Things could most definitely be worse.

Scout finishes up and rushes toward us, ready to go back inside, too.

He goes straight for the blankets I'd arranged on the floor and flops down on them.

"Hey, Mister," I tell the dog. "What makes you think that's your bed?"

Scout just looks at me with big puppy dog eyes.

"He's think you're a sucker," Lucas says.

"I guess I am," I say as I sit down next to the dog. "At least maybe we can share."

Scout actually seems delighted to share the makeshift bed. I settle in and he puts his head on my lap.

"And she stole my dog," Lucas says.

I smile up at Lucas who's sitting on an old wooden chair, sketching on a drafting pad.

I don't say anything, but I wonder, maybe even hope, if maybe he might be just a little bit jealous of his dog.

Chapter Eight

Lucas

As the sun sets over the mountain tops, I go outside to bring in another load of firewood.

It's still snowing and the temperature has definitely dropped a little more.

It's almost time to walk back to the diner to get dinner. I hope Madison isn't one of those girls who needs something different to eat at every meal. I've dated girls like that. The ones who like a variety, always wanting to try something new.

Personally, when I find something I like I can eat it every day. When I was a college student, I ate spaghetti every day for lunch for two years. Two years. I never got tired of it.

Then I moved back to the ranch and my family broke that up.

If Madison needs variety, she's going to be hurting. Mel doesn't have spaghetti, even though he has a decent menu, but since he cooks everything himself, he doesn't branch out much.

I spend a few minutes outside making sure all my tools are put away for the night. Lock up my truck. Not necessary, but a habit. And watch the splash of pinks across the sky as the sun drops behind the mountains. Nature's sand mandala. Every day the world creates a beautiful sunset lasting only moments, letting go of the beauty that returns in a few hours as a brand new day full of promise.

Tomorrow, after I check out the avalanche damage, I'll call my family and give them the news. They've probably heard about the avalanche by now, but they don't know I'm here. They probably think I'm in Denver wasting time.

If they only knew. I'm here. Trying to do my part to save the family ranch.

I refuse to tell them until it actually happens. Until I get the cabin renovated and it sells. This way, in the event that the project falls through somewhere, I don't have to deal with disappointing them. If it works like I hope it does, it'll be a pleasant surprise.

With everything secure for the night, I go back inside where my dog is curled up on the blankets with Madison.

Although she's reading, she looks like she's about half asleep.

I decide to surprise her with some hot cocoa.

I might not have a stove, but I do have an electric tea kettle and some hot cocoa packets.

It doesn't take long to heat the water and stir in the hot chocolate mix.

"I don't have any marshmallows," I say, kneeling next to her and handing her a steaming mug of hot chocolate. "But you might like this."

She straightens up and smiles. "You made hot chocolate."

"I think I heard you mention that you want to drink hot chocolate in front of the fireplace."

She takes a cautious sip. "It's just one of those Christmassy things people do when it snows," she says. "In my imagination."

I stretch out my legs. "And what else do people do in your imagination when it snows at Christmas?"

"They make cookies."

"I can't help you there. Not without a stove."

"It's okay."

"What else?" I sip the hot chocolate and decide it needs to cool before I can drink it.

"A Christmas tree," she says.

"We can do that, but I don't have any decorations."

"Do you have popcorn?"

"I think I can get some. Mel has a microwave."

"We can string it up and use it for decorations. Get some pinecones. We can make origami decorations, too."

"You do origami?" I ask, feeling a little concerned that this just got complicated.

"No. But we can look it up."

"No Internet."

"Oh. Right."

Even though I'm relieved that I'm not going to have to suffer through learning to do origami, I hate seeing that disappointed look on her face and would do just about anything to avoid it. "But," I say. "We can make paper chains."

Her face lights up again. "We did that as kids. We just need construction paper and some glue."

"Are you hungry?" I ask. "We can go by the store on our way to dinner and see what kind of supplies we can find." I glance at my watch. "We have to leave soon, though, if we're going to get there before they close."

"Do we have time to finish our hot chocolate?" she asks.

"Sure. We'll make time."

"So tomorrow we'll go out and cut down a tree," she says. "Christmas Eve is in two days."

"You're not upset that you most probably going to miss being in Alpine Falls for Christmas?"

"I'm not upset about it so much as I hate to disappoint-ment my friends. They were counting on me and I don't like it they're probably worried about me."

"What happened to your cell phone?"

"Dropped it right onto the concrete in an El Paso parking lot. Must have hit just right."

"Must have. I drop my phone all the time."

"I do, too. I should have stopped to replace it, but it always takes hours to do something like that."

"Coulda. Woulda. Shoulda. Life is full of them."

"You're not kidding," she agrees. "This is good, but speaking of shoulds, we should go , shouldn't we? I don't want the store to close on us."

"You're right. I'll just take that mug." I set them aside and hold out a hand. "Can I help you up?"

She puts her hand in mine and I pull her to her feet. Scout gets up, too, and shakes off the nap he'd been indulging in.

"Scout is always ready to go," I say.

"A sign of a good dog."

"The fire looks okay," I say, spreading the ashes around to make sure. The last thing I need is for the cabin to burn down.

We put on our coats and head out into the snow.

I have to admit, even for a jaded local, used to the snow, it's all quite charming.

But it's not the snow.

It's the delightful girl walking along beside me.

Chapter Nine

Madison

Somehow no one in town has a phonebook.

"People take them for artifacts," Mel says. "They sell them online."

"Why would they do that?" I ask.

"Anything for a buck," Mel says. "What can I get you to eat?"

"Let us take a minute to study the menu," Lucas says.

"If you don't have the menu memorized by now," Mel says. "I'm worried about you."

Lucas gives him a scathing look. "I'm not the only one here, am I?"

Mel shrugs and walks back to the kitchen.

"He seems grouchy," I say, leaning forward to whisper to Lucas.

"He is. Always. But he's a good cook."

"I guess that makes up for his grouchiness," I say, but I'm not so sure. "Are you planning on putting in an oven?"

"So now you want to start cooking," Lucas says.

"Just making conversation," I say, looking over the menu that wouldn't take any time at all to memorize.

"I actually have one on order."

"Well, so much for those plans," I say. "We have hurricanes. You have avalanches."

"At least you get some warning for hurricanes," he says.

"Usually. That is true."

Scout is sitting on the floor on one side of us and we have bags of supplies we got from the store on the other side. I never thought I'd be so happy to find a pack of construction paper, scissors, and a glue stick.

I might be stuck out here in the middle of nowhere for Christmas, but that doesn't mean we can't have the little cabin looking at least a little bit festive.

"Do you know what you want?" Lucas asks.

"The tuna sandwich and fries."

"Good choice. I'll have that, too." He holds up a hand and after getting Mel's attention, relays our order.

"Why doesn't he hire some help?" I ask.

"I guess he doesn't think he needs it."

"I guess. It just seems a little weird having one person doing everything."

"You have to remember that there aren't that many

people coming in. In fact, I think I'm his only regular when I'm in town."

"Good point." Especially since there aren't any other customers in the diner at the moment. "Is your family expecting you for Christmas?"

"Of course. I'll call them in the morning after I check out the damage from the avalanche. Tell them I'm not going to make it."

"If they happen to know Hannah and Jack, ask them to let them know I'm not going to make the wedding."

Lucas just looks blankly at me. Seconds pass. "Hannah and Jack Thompson?" he finally asks.

"That's his last name. I couldn't remember. Wait. You know them?"

"You could say that," he says.

"Oh. Wow. Do you think you could get a message to them?"

"Madison," he says. "Jack is my brother."

Chapter Ten

Lucas

MADISON IS LOOKING at me as though I've lost a marble. I'm probably looking about the same at her.

"So you're Hannah's friend. The one coming up from Houston for the wedding."

"Yes. And you're one of Jack's brothers."

"Yes."

"That's all I know about you. Hannah hasn't told me anything else. Just that Jack has two brothers."

"That kind of figures," I say. "They don't see me much."

"Why not?"

"I guess because I spend a lot of time here." I don't tell

her that I live in an apartment over the barn at my family's ranch. That I don't spend a lot of time over at the house.

"That and she's overly preoccupied with Jack."

"I've never known two people to be more preoccupied with each other," I say. "Except maybe my parents. They're pretty much that way, too."

"I guess that's where Jack gets it."

"I suppose so."

"You don't take after your parents?"

"Not in that way. Trenton, that's my other brother, swears I was adopted."

She smiles. "Were you?"

"Hardly. Our mother will box anyone's ears who even hints at that."

"Your mother sounds like a tough woman."

"She is. She and Dad have worked really hard taking care of that ranch. After Dad's accident, though, she just sort of shifted everything over to Jack."

"What about your other brother? Trenton?"

"Trenton? He's an architect and lives in Boulder. He's not interested in the ranch life."

"That's too bad."

"Why do you say that?"

"No reason," she says with a little shrug. "It's just that it's a family business and it seems like everyone would want to pitch in."

"Yeah. It does, doesn't it?"

She's not wrong. Mucking stalls has never been my thing, but I'm doing my part now. In my own way. Or at least I'm trying to. I'm just crossing my fingers that this cabin venture pays off.

The avalanche has definitely put a damper on things.

Madison leans back in her chair. "I feel so much better now."

"How is that?"

"For one thing, you'll be able to let Hannah know where I am. So that's a relief. And the other thing is selfish on my part."

"Now you have to tell me."

"I don't feel so bad about being the only one to miss the wedding."

"Misery loves company."

"It's not that," she says. "It's almost like you're part of the family. And if we're stuck here in the middle of nowhere, at least I—."

"Hey." Mel stops at our table and sets our plates in front of us. "Be careful about your comments."

"Sorry," she says, looking up at the grouchy old man. "But you've got to admit that it's kind of true."

Mel shrugs and walks away. "Anyway," she finishes her thought. "I don't feel so alone."

"Me either," I say, looking into her deep green eyes.

She smiles before dipping a French fry in ketchup.

Who would have thought I'd meet the most charming woman ever right here in the little town of Luchara?

Chapter Eleven

Madison

Lucas is quite ingenuous. He brought a set of sawhorses inside and balanced a piece of plywood over the top of them to make a table.

We pull up the two wooden chairs on either side of the table and get to work on making our Christmas decorations.

"I may have to find somewhere else to sleep," I say.

"Why is that?" Lucas asks as he sorts through the construction paper, pulling out all the Christmas colors, not just red and green, but blue and white and gray.

"Scout has taken over my bed."

"You can't blame him. It's the best seat in the house."

"I guess after you get it renovated, you'll buy some furniture," I say.

"Maybe," he says as he takes the glue out of the package.

"You think the avalanche is going to turn Luchara into a ghost town," I say in response to his noncommittal response.

"I hope not." He looks at me with something akin to horror.

"Sorry. You just seem like you're worried about it."

"I am worried about it. How wide are we going to make the strips?"

"I don't know. I think part of the charm is having them uneven."

"Maybe when we were seven," he says. "I think we should measure them out. Maybe half an inch."

"Okay then. You measure and cut. I'll glue."

He takes a ruler and starts measuring off half inch strips.

"You were serious?"

"We don't want our tree looking like a child decorated it."

I give him a look. "They're paper strips. They aren't going to exactly look like designer décor."

"Good point. Still. I prefer to measure."

"Okay." While he measures, I walk over to the kitchen counter and fill a bowl with popcorn Mel popped for us and bring it to our table.

"I thought that was for decoration," he says as I pick up a handful and start eating it.

"It would be if we had a needle and thread."

"Ah ha," he says. "But I've been thinking about that. I

found some fishing line in a box and there's a fish hook that we can use as a needle."

I drop the uneaten popcorn back into the bowl. "Now you tell me."

"I actually just thought of it," he says with a disarming grin that sends butterflies slamming about in my stomach.

"Are you sure you don't want me to cut some of those?"

"Okay. But I hope you have a steady hand," he says, sliding a piece of red construction paper with precise lines in my direction.

I pick up the scissors and start cutting. "Are you sure you aren't an architect?" I ask.

"I'm sure. That's my brother's thing. So Trenton got a degree in architecture. Jack majored in aviation. And I, believe it or not, majored in psychology."

"Psychology?" I stop cutting and study him. "I would not have guessed that."

"Yeah well. Turns out it's not worth much as an under-graduate degree. Takes advanced degrees to do anything with it."

"You didn't want to get an advanced degree?"

"Nope." He keeps his gaze down, focused on drawing exact lines over a piece of green paper. "My plan was to play football."

"Now that I can see. Did you play in college?"

"I did. It's actually the whole reason I went to college. But I didn't make the pros."

"I'm sorry."

"It's okay. I don't think I would've cared much for the lifestyle."

I go back to cutting strips. "So you decided to become a handyman instead."

"I've been learning construction since I was a kid following my uncle around. It was either that or muck out stalls."

"I'm not sure what that is, but it doesn't sound like something I'd want to do either."

"You wouldn't like it."

I take the cap off the stick of glue and secure two ends of one of the paper strips together.

Holding it up, I frown at it. "I think we're going to have to make these strips smaller."

"You want a small chain?"

"I think it would look better, don't you? Let's try it." I pick up the scissors and snip one of the strips in half then glue the ends. "Better?"

Lucas takes his ruler and draws a mark down the middle of the paper he's currently measuring out. "Done," he says.

"You're funny."

"Yeah. Well. That's what my family keeps saying. But they don't mean it as a compliment."

He keeps his face down, making it hard for me to see his expression, but I don't have to be a psychologist to sense the hurt he's feeling.

"Your family is wrong," I say. They're wrong about him. And right now I'm thinking maybe it's a good thing that I'm the one who gets to spend Christmas with Lucas.

If his family doesn't understand him, then I'm the lucky one.

Chapter Twelve

Lucas

"I THINK we're good for the night," I say, stretching a blanket out onto the floor. "We've got three sleeping areas. With Scout in the middle."

"He snagged the best spot," Madison says.

"That's okay. He's acting chaperone for the evening."

Madison grins. "Funny."

"We've got plenty of firewood and the little heater behind us."

"It's nice and warm. As long as we don't lose power, we should be good. Does the power ever go out up here?"

"I have no idea," I say. "I hope not."

"At least we have a candle and a flashlight."

"So… do you want me to let you sleep in or do you want to get up early and walk to the diner for coffee?"

"Does coffee include breakfast?"

"It can. I don't think Mel ever leaves the diner."

"Then I'm in."

"A breakfast girl. Interesting."

"What? You have something against breakfast?"

"Breakfast is my favorite meal of the day."

"I can't tell if you're being serious." She carefully arranges the paper garland which looks surprisingly good. She calls it ombre, keeping like colors together with an elaborate plan to wrap them artfully around the tree we're going out tomorrow to chop down.

"I would never jest about breakfast," I say.

"Good to know," she says, stifling a yawn.

I add a log to the fireplace and use an iron poker to rearrange the logs.

"We have a big day ahead of us tomorrow," I say.

"Yes. About that. I'd like to walk with you down to the avalanche area."

"Sure. We should see what the weather's doing though before we plan to go very far."

"Okay," she says, obviously disappointed.

"I have an extra pair of boots in the truck," I say. "We can try lacing them up really tight. See if you can walk in them."

"Okay," she says, with a smile. "Just wondering. Does the shower work?"

"It's not much to look at, but it works just fine."

"Good. I'd like to shower before we start our day."

"I'll wake you up early. Walk to the diner to get us coffee while you shower. Then we'll walk back to the diner for breakfast and on to the avalanche area."

"Then we'll go chop down our tree."

"Yes. I suppose we'll go chop down a tree."

"You still have hope that we'll get out of here," she says.

"Even though I know better, yes, I guess I do. I've never missed Christmas with my family."

"Then we need to manifest a miracle," she says.

I don't know about manifesting a miracle, but I do know that we'll find a way out of here. I just haven't figured out exactly what that way will be yet.

Chapter Thirteen

Madison

I honestly hadn't thought I'd be able to sleep in a strange place with a stranger sleeping just a few feet away.

But with the distant roar of the rushing river outside and the gentle crackling of the fire in the fireplace and, Scout's soft snoring, I soon find myself drifting off.

Lucas has been nothing less than a perfect gentleman.

And especially now that I know he's practically family, I expect no less. His brother is marrying one of my two best friends. Hannah. I haven't known Hannah nearly as long as I've known Olivia, but Olivia and I just sort of took Hannah into our fold and now she's one of us.

So she's family and that means Lucas is family.

I hate to miss Hannah's wedding, even if she is already technically married to Jack. She thought they were divorced for ten years, but not Jack. Jack waited for her. For ten years.

I wonder just how long he really would have waited. Maybe he knew Hannah would show up one day looking for divorce papers so she could get remarried. It's hard to say.

Whatever he was thinking, his steadfastness to Hannah is like nothing I've ever heard of.

I only met Jack once. Briefly. At a pizza place in Houston. It was months ago. Long enough ago that I don't remember him enough to really compare him to Lucas.

I do remember that he was good looking and Lucas definitely shares that family trait.

Lucas is not only good looking, he's good hearted. He's been going out of his way to make me happy.

He made me hot chocolate, even if it wasn't very good. I'd never tell him. It's the thought that counts and our situation doesn't allow for much.

He set up a table and helped me make Christmas decorations for a tree we don't have yet.

And he's keeping a warm fire going.

I have to admit that I'm quite charmed by him.

Before I know it, I'm drifting off and the next thing I know, I hear Lucas talking to me.

"Good morning, Sunshine," he says. At first I think I must be dreaming, but I pry my eyes open enough to see him kneeling in front of me.

I stretch beneath the warm blankets and try to decide if

it's morning with nothing to go on other than the soft glow of the flames in the hearth.

"I had to take Scout outside," he says. "So I went ahead and picked up coffee."

"Coffee in bed," I say, sitting up. "Doesn't get much better than that."

After he hands me one of the paper cups, I take a sip. "Perfect," I say and I mean it.

"I figured anyone who likes hot chocolate would like a latte."

"You figured right," I say, enjoying the hot coffee.

He sits down on his pallet, but Scout decides he wants to share mine again.

"Good morning, Scout," I say. "Did you have a good walk?"

"He made snow angels."

"You did not," I say, rubbing Scout's head. "Is it still snowing?" I look toward the window, but it's still too dark to tell.

"Not right now, but it's a winter wonderland out there."

"Oh. I can't wait to see it."

"Get your shower and put on some warm clothes. It's not going anywhere anytime soon."

"That bad, huh?"

"I brought these boots in for you to try." He holds up a pair of well-worn, broken-in boots. "If we were in Alpine Falls, I'd know exactly where you could get boots."

"It's okay. After I get showered and dressed, I'll try them. Thank you. For the coffee and the boots."

"Don't mention it. Did you sleep well?"

"I guess I did. I didn't even really know I'd fallen asleep until I heard you talking."

"I hate waking someone up when they're sleeping," he says. "But I'm a man of my word and I told you I'd wake you up."

"What about you? Did you sleep well?"

"I always sleep well here. It's just amazingly quiet and peaceful."

"Coming from the man who grew up in a quaint little small town."

"How do you know it's quaint?"

"Hannah told me."

The hot coffee has me awake and now that I'm awake, I'm ready to get the day started. Lucas and I have a big day planned. For two people stranded in the middle of nowhere, we have a long to-do list.

Chapter Fourteen

Lucas

THE AVALANCHE AREA is worse than I expected. It literally wiped away any signs that the road was ever even there. Instead of a road alongside a mountain, there's nothing there but, well, the side of a mountain with a ton of it, dirt and rocks, mostly lying in a pile at the bottom of the canyon.

The state police is there with a couple of engineers and they won't let us anywhere near the area.

Madison, wearing her white wool coat with a festive scarf in Christmas red, stands next to me, looking quite frankly, a little ill. She has one hand on Scout's collar. I guess so maybe he won't try to dash off into the rubble.

She looks rather cute wearing my boots, way too big for her. Just knowing that she's wearing my boots gives me a warm feeling inside.

"It's going to be okay," I say, feeling the need to comfort even as I knew the words are empty.

The avalanche was bad. If there wasn't a little village on the other side of it, it would easily have become one of those roads that never gets repaired. In fact, it might anyway. They might figure out a way to get everyone out and let it go. Call it a loss.

In the event that happens, some people will never recover financially. My situation isn't good, but I'll recover. My cabin is an investment project, not something I've put my whole life into.

Like Mel. If forced to abandon his diner, what will become of him. Him and the other merchants?

I angle my thoughts around, away from the worst case scenario and try to focus on the positive. There's no sign of anyone being hurt.

Things could have been so very worse.

"What do we do?" Madison asks.

"We do our thing and let them do theirs. They'll let us know when they have it figured out."

"Is there a way for us to hike out of here?" she asks.

"I don't know. But I do know that they'll figure something out. There are too many lives at stake for them not to."

"We should go and call Hannah and Jack," she says. "Let them know we aren't going to make their wedding tomorrow."

"I guess there's no time like the present to get it over with."

"They'll understand," she says. "I know we don't have Internet, but can you take some photos with your phone and send them to me when I get my phone replaced?"

"Sure." I pull my phone out of my pocket and snap some shots of the avalanche area.

"It's so pretty here," she says wistfully.

"Beautiful, but deadly," I say.

The walk back to town isn't long. I'm still surprised no one heard the avalanche. I guess everyone was just going about their business, not paying any attention to the outside world. Probably listening to music or television or talking on their phones. It just went unnoticed.

And small propeller airplane passes overhead, flying low, as we walk back to town.

"Reporters?" Madison asks.

"Maybe. Or someone just out taking a look."

Back at the general store to use the phone, everyone wants to see the photos.

And everyone is talking about what's going to happen next.

The old timers are saying Lachara will become a ghost town after they get everyone out.

The younger people are hopeful that the road can somehow be repaired.

The few tourists just want to get out. They don't care what happens.

Me? I'm a little torn. On the one hand, I really want to

get out of here and get home to my family for Christmas and my brother's wedding.

But on the other hand, I'm enjoying spending time with Madison. Under normal circumstances, she and I would probably never have gotten to know each other like this.

We would have simply been introduced, then we would have gone our separate ways. She would have hung out with her friends, Hannah and Olivia. And I would have minded my own business, whatever that happened to be at the time.

Even in the midst of a disastrous situation, I can't help but think that this avalanche, somehow, was good.

Chapter Fifteen

Madison

Both Hannah and Olivia both get on the phone with me after Lucas tells Jack what happened.

"I'm so glad you're okay," Hannah says to me then she says to Olivia. "I told you we should have checked on her while we were in Houston."

"It's okay," I say. "You wouldn't have found me no matter what you did."

"I just can't believe you ended up in the same place as Lucas," Olivia says. "He wasn't supposed to be there and you weren't supposed to be there. It's just so strange."

"It's fate," Hannah says.

Looking across the room at Lucas, I send him a helpless expression. He just smiles.

He's standing next to a stand of paperbacks, flipping through one book, then another, looking for something to read since I guess I took his book yesterday. Scout is sitting at his feet.

Maybe it is fate. Or coincidence. Or accidental.

Whatever it is, I'm not complaining.

"Look," I say. "I'm on somebody's landline, probably running up a big phone bill for long-distance."

"Is that a thing?" Olivia asks.

"Yes," Hannah says. "Remember where you are."

"I just wanted to let you know I'm okay and I'll be there when I can. If I can. I'm not going to make the wedding and I'm sorry about that."

"It can't be helped," Hannah says. "Just take care of yourself."

"I will. I love you both."

"We love you, too. Merry Christmas!"

I put the receiver down to disconnect the line.

Squaring my shoulders, I walk over to join Lucas.

"How did Jack take the news?" I ask.

"After he got past the part about being confused about me being here, he actually thought it was a little funny. Not the avalanche part. But the part about you ending up here. Staying in my cabin."

"Yeah. The girls kind of had a hard time with that one, too."

We walk outside. "Too early for lunch," he says. "Feel like going to look for a tree?"

"Sure."

"Boots holding up okay?"

"Not bad." I send him a little smile. I like knowing that I'm wearing his boots, even if they are way too big for me. "Olivia said something that struck me as a little odd."

"Yeah. What's that?" he asks as we veer down the path leading to his cabin, freshly fallen snow crunching beneath our boots.

"She said you aren't supposed to be here."

"They didn't know where I was," he says.

"They don't know about the cabin?" I ask carefully.

"They do not."

I wait for him to volunteer more. Scout runs ahead, then disappears into the trees and comes up behind us.

"He likes doing that, doesn't he?" I ask.

"Yes. He's a little crazy sometimes."

"He's cute."

"When I was in college playing football," Lucas says, picking up a stick and tossing it ahead of Scout. "I'd go for weeks without talking to my family. They had no idea where I was or what I was doing."

"You were busy," I say.

"I was actually a little wild. They got used to it." He looks unseeing off into the distance. "They still think of me as being irresponsible and they don't expect much out of me."

Scout brings the stick back and drops it at Lucas's feet. "I didn't know you could do that," Lucas tells him.

"But you are responsible. You're working."

"Sort of," he says. "Wait here while I get the axe."

I wait while he gets an axe out of a tool cabinet in the back of his truck.

As he tosses the axe over his shoulder, we start walking again, behind the cabin now.

"I bought this cabin," he says. "for the purpose of fixing it up and selling it for a profit."

"So you're flipping it?" I'm a bit impressed now and things are starting to make sense. Like his lack of commitment in buying furniture.

"Yeah. No point in keeping it a secret anyone. No one's going to buy a cabin they can't drive to."

"You never know," I say.

"I was planning to sell it and use the money to help out around the ranch. My way of helping out the family," he says.

"Why didn't you tell them?" I ask as we reach the rushing river and walk alongside it.

"Because in the event it didn't work, they'd just see it as me making a bad decision."

"I don't know," I say, carefully stepping onto a boulder at the water's edge. "I think they would appreciate the effort."

"Maybe," he says. "I guess I wasn't willing to take that chance. It's a moot point now."

"There," I say, pointing across the river. "There's our tree."

"I'm sure there are plenty of trees on this side of the river," he says.

"But that one's perfect," I say.

He mutters something about women beneath his breath, but I see the smile on his face.

He doesn't need to know that I did that one purpose. To distract him.

And it worked.

Chapter Sixteen

Lucas

"You really want that tree?" I ask. "The one across the river?"

"It looks perfect from here," Madison says.

I can't tell if she's being difficult on purpose or if she's messing with me.

Doesn't much matter so much. If the tree she wants is across the river, that's the tree I'm going to get for her.

"Come on, then," I say.

"Where are we going?"

"You'll see."

It's an extra quarter mile around, but definitely worth it.

"We're going to walk across this bridge," I say. "then see if we can find that tree again."

"Everything does all kind of start to blend together," she says.

We walk across the little wooden bridge and backtrack to the area where we'd seen the tree.

"Is this it?" I ask, stopping in front of a blue spruce tree.

She looks back across the river. I know she has no idea.

Not with the snow on the ground.

"Yes," she says.

"How do you know?"

She puts a hand over her eyes. "I see our footprints across the river. That's where we turned around."

"Impressive. Very impressive. There's hope for you city girl after all."

She smiles. "Never underestimate a Houston girl."

"You sure this is the one you want?" I ask, walking around it. "It's too tall for the cabin."

"That's okay. You can cut the bottom off of it. Right?"

"Sure," I say. "Why not?"

"How does this work?" she asks.

"You have to take Scout and stand back."

"Okay. How far?"

"Next to the river would be good."

"Come on Scout." She taps her leg and Scout happily follows.

When I deem her far enough away to be safe, I go about the business of chopping down the tree. It crashes to the ground right where I planned.

Now for the hard part. Getting the tree back to the cabin.

Picking up the tree trunk, I start dragging it.

"Can I help?" Madison asks.

"Just lead the way," I say. "I'll follow you."

"And I'll follow Scout."

Scout is ahead of both of us.

"He's just hungry," I say.

"I'm a little hungry, too," she says, walking along beside me.

"It's the fresh mountain air."

"It must be because I don't eat much."

"We'll fix that," I say.

"Until Mel runs out of food."

"Good point. Someone will drop in food. Too many people here for them to ignore."

"What if it was just us?" she asks.

"What do you mean?"

"What would they do if we were the only ones on this side of the avalanche? Would they drop us food?"

"They would probably evacuate us."

"Then why don't they just evacuate everyone?" she asks.

"I guess they have to figure it out."

With me still dragging the tree, we cross the bridge and follow the trail back to the cabin. We walk in silence, each lost in our own thoughts.

Since I can only deal with what I know, I contemplate how I'm going to cut the tree so that it fits inside the cabin.

There's a pitched area of the ceiling in one corner that will add a couple of feet if we put the tree there.

"There's someone at our door," Madison says, slowing down.

Pulling myself out of my thoughts, I look up to see the cabin just coming into view. Sure enough. There are two men standing at the door.

Chapter Seventeen

Madison

I TAMP down my annoyance at having someone disturb my time with Lucas.

I've accepted the fact that I'm going to be spending Christmas here in Luchara with Lucas.

Accepted and now I'm looking forward to it.

Two men waiting for us at the door of our cabin was not in my equation.

Lucas quietly drops the tree, leaving it behind before they see us.

"Do you know them?" I whisper.

"No," he says, keeping his eyes on them.

"Should we be worried?"

"No," he says, squaring his shoulders.

The two guys see us now, so we stop talking. Lucas walks slightly in front of me as though ready to shield me in an instant.

"Can I help you?" he asks.

The two men are dressed in work clothes beneath heavy down coats and carrying clips boards in their hands. They're wearing hard hats over wool caps. They're dressed a lot like the engineers we saw out at the avalanche area to me, but I don't think they're the same people.

"This your place?" the older one asks. Both men are wearing beards and the younger one is wearing glasses.

"It is."

"My name is Ralph and this here is Teddy. We're canvasing the area to get a firm count on how many people are stranded up here."

"How did you get in here?" Lucas asks.

"Parachuted," the younger man says.

"Well, there's just the two of us," Lucas says. "And my dog."

"Can we get your names?" Teddy asks, ready to write on his clipboard.

Lucas hesitates, but then tells them. It's not that they couldn't just ask someone anyway.

"Lucas Thompson and Madison." He looks at me.

"Lane," I say. "Madison Lane."

"And Scout," Lucas says, putting a hand on Scout's collar.

"How many days do you estimate your supplies will last?" Teddy reads the next question off his list.

"Don't have any," Lucas says. "We're using the diner."

The two men look at each other.

"Do you need anything in the immediate future?" Ralph asks, putting a stop to Teddy's list of questions.

"Depends on what you call the immediate future."

"Now," Ralph says. "Looks like you're safe for the moment."

"I'd say we are."

"We'll get out of your hair, then", Ralph says. "Here's my card if you need anything."

"Don't have cell phone service," Lucas says, not moving.

"Well. Right. I'll just leave it here." Ralph sticks the business card into the door jamb. "Take care now."

We watch as they turn and walk away. We watch them until they disappear around a curve in the road.

"You don't trust them," I say.

"Don't know them. They didn't show us any identification."

I don't bother to mention that he didn't ask, but I get what he's saying. There are scammers everywhere. Not just in the city.

"I'll get our tree," he says. "Make sure Scout doesn't run after them."

I wrap my fingers around Scout's collar and wonder how I could keep a dog as big as a horse from doing anything he wanted to do.

Chapter Eighteen

Lucas

APPARENTLY MY OVERCAUTIOUSNESS WAS ILL-FOUNDED. Ralph and Teddy have been making the rounds, getting everyone's information. They're with some state agency or another.

"What do you think they're going to do?" I ask Mel.

It's the middle of the afternoon and we're the only ones left in the diner after a busy lunch time.

Mel slings a dishcloth over his shoulder. "Not a damn thing."

"Well somebody has to do something," I say.

Madison and I are sitting on two barstools at Mel's counter. He doesn't usually keep barstools out, but with the avalanche and everyone coming in to get information and a little food to go along with it, he had to pull out some more seating.

Mel flips over a hamburger patty sizzling on the grill. "They don't care. What they might do is drop off a few supplies."

"Then how do you propose we all get out of here?"

"I guess I'll be staying."

"Mel," I say with a glance at Madison. "You're going to run out of supplies. What are you going to do?"

"If it comes to that, I'll live off the land."

"Is there another road?" Madison asks, hopefully.

"One way in. One way out," Mel says.

"What about a trail?"

"Not unless you can scale the side of a mountain." Mel flips the burger again.

"I guess that answers that question," I say to Madison.

"I guess it does." She sits back looking a little defeated.

"You hungry?" Mel asks.

We both shake our heads. Mel proceeds to put the hamburger together, then sits down in front of us and proceeds to eat. There's a first time for everything.

"Do you have a map?" I ask him.

Mel reaches under the counter and slaps a dogeared paper map onto the counter.

I spread it out in front of us and get my bearings. Lachera is the perfect place for people to escape and get away from it all.

Until it isn't.

Madison looks over my shoulder. "What about that road right there?" she asks.

Mel shakes his head and doesn't even bother to look up.

"I don't think that's a road," I say.

"There really isn't any way out of here is there?" she asks.

"Doesn't look like it."

Mel finishes off his burger and gets up to start cleaning the grill. The man never takes a break.

"I think," I say. "We just need to go back. Decorate our tree and enjoy Christmas as best we can. Nothing's going to happen until after Christmas anyway."

She nods and forces a little smile.

"Hey," I say. "It's what we planned anyway, remember? We do have the perfect tree."

"You're right," she says, straightening. "It'll all work out."

"Of course it will." I put a hand over hers and gently squeeze it.

I get it that she's a little afraid. But we have everything we need for right now.

We may not get out of here in time for Christmas, but we'll get out in due time.

No matter what Mel says, I have faith in that.

Chapter Nineteen

Madison

On the walk home, with Scout leading the way, I find myself thinking about too many things at one time.

"Penny for your thoughts," Lucas says.

"Really? Okay. But promise you won't laugh."

"Why not? Is it funny?"

"No. It's not funny." I elbow him. "If you laugh, I won't tell you anything else."

"I won't laugh. Scout's honor."

I narrow my eyes at him. "Where you a boy scout?"

"Yes."

I look at him sideways.

"Honest. I was."

"Okay. I was wondering what would happen if we never get out of here. What if we're stuck here for the rest of our lives and we grow old here?"

He laughs out loud.

"You promised you wouldn't laugh." I put my hands on my hips and glare at him.

"I'm sorry. But it's funny."

"How is it funny? Seriously? What if we're stuck here?"

"If we're stuck here, then we'll have a passel of beautiful children."

My eyes widen, wondering how he got to that exactly. "Presumptuous much?"

"No. But if we're stuck here, it'll be like being on a deserted island. We'll be forced to… I mean." He smiles a bit rakishly and I have to admit I get a funny feeling in my stomach. "What else are we going to do?"

"Okay. Let's decorate our tree. Enjoy Christmas in the quiet forest. And know that somehow they'll miraculously rebuild the road in no time."

"Exactly. We follow the plan."

"The plan," I say with a little shake of my head.

"What?"

"It's just funny. I have my life planned out on a spreadsheet."

"Now you're purposely trying to be funny."

"I'm not being funny. I really do have a spreadsheet. Mostly career. I was thinking maybe it's time to make some changes. But… this… this is a little off in left field from what I was thinking."

"Being stranded in the mountains?"

"Yes. With no technology. It's hard to make a career change without the Internet."

"Oh. I don't know. There's a lot you could do."

"Like what?" Scout races up behind us.

"Like we could raise puppies and sell them."

That's unsettlingly close to what I do right now. "Who would we sell them to?"

"We'd have to barter them to the other people who are stuck here."

"Okay. Not exactly profitable. What else do you have?"

"You could make origami?"

"And how exactly would that be profitable?" I ask.

"We could box it up and send it out with drones."

I stop walking and just stand there looking at him.

"I think we need to figure a way to hike out of here."

He runs a hand along the side of his truck. "I sure do hate to give up my truck," he says.

"Do you think insurance will cover our vehicles?" I ask, looking at my own car.

"There's probably a clause in there about abandonment."

"You're probably right."

He unlocks the front door to the cabin and I follow Scout inside, flipping on the light as I go. Lucas turns on the little heater and starts laying a fire in the fireplace.

I sit down on my blanket. "All I know is it's good to be home."

Chapter Twenty

Lucas

I GLANCE over my shoulder at Madison. She's lying back on her blanket, her eyes closed.

I don't think she even realized what she just said.

She'd called this little cabin home.

I'd laughed at her being worried about us being stuck here and growing old. I'd laughed because it was funny.

It's not going to happen.

The thing is I can think of worst ways to spend a life than spending it stranded here in the mountains with Madison. Far worse ways.

It won't happen though. I have some ideas. They just aren't fleshed out well enough to share them.

After I get a fire going, I leave Madison napping and go outside to cut the bottom off the tree. I use a hand saw because it's quieter than a chain saw even if it is a whole lot slower.

After I have what I think is a good height for it, I saw off some of the bottom limbs and open the door to drag it inside.

Madison sits up, pushing her hair out of her face, looking all sleepy.

"Good nap?" I ask.

"I wasn't sleeping," she says.

"No? Okay. I might need your help making sure I get this tree standing up straight."

"You already cut the bottom off." She stands up and stretches.

There are definitely worse things than being stuck out her with her. In fact, right now I'm having trouble thinking of anything better.

"We have to get this thing up and decorated," I say. "Tomorrow is Christmas Eve."

"We should go into town," she says. "And buy some presents to wrap up. Put them under the tree."

"That's a good idea," I say. "It's a great idea, actually."

She grins. "We definitely have to get presents for Scout."

"And each other."

"That might be a little more difficult. I think the shelves are going to be bare pretty quickly."

"We'll find something. And if we don't, we'll make something. We still have construction paper and glue."

"I still don't know origami."

"It's okay," I say, tightening the screws that will hold the tree in the stand we'd bought at the general store.

"We don't have lights," she says.

"Not necessary. We're having an old-fashioned Christmas."

"An old-fashioned Christmas. I like that."

"Here goes," I say, standing the tree upright. "How does it look?"

"It looks perfect," she says, clasping her hands together.

I slide one of the wooden chair over and climb up. "Hand me whichever of those paper chains you want to put on top."

She hands me the yellow one. I wrap it around the top of the tree.

"I have a challenge for you," I say.

"What's that? I'm always up for a challenge."

"Figure out what you want to make for a tree topper."

"Like a star?"

"Yes. Like a star. What color goes next?"

She hands me the pale green chain and I wrap it around the tree.

"We're getting somewhere," I say.

"It's going to look good," she says. "No matter what people might say."

"Who could possibly make fun of our tree? It's a lovely blue spruce. And I take offense to any criticism."

"Me too."

She hands me the gray chain next.

"I think this ombre thing is going to work."

"You had doubts?" she asks.

"None to speak of."

"I think that means yes."

"Nah. I trust you." I climb off the chair. "What's next?"

We finish up with dark blue paper chains at the bottom.

"We forgot to do the popcorn," she says.

"I thought we'd make those next."

We settle down at our plywood table, the big bowl of popcorn between us, and I hand her a fishing line with a hook I straightened on the end.

"Have you ever done this before?" I ask.

"Honestly," she says. "No. Actually this thing looks a bit dangerous," she says as she examines the rusty fish hook.

"Maybe I should do that part," I say. "There's no ER in Lachera. You can be in charge of making sure things don't get tangled up."

"I think I can handle it," she says, but she hands me the ugly-looking hook anyway.

"Besides," I say. "You have to work on the tree-topper."

"Right." She glances back at the tree, then slides the stack of construction paper toward her. "What color are you thinking?"

"You're in charge of that part."

"Red," she says. "We have one piece of red left."

"Red it is. We really need a video on how to string up this popcorn."

"How hard can it be? Just stab it through the middle."

"You make things sound so easy."

She smiles and my heart melts.

I know that no matter what it is, if she wants me to do something, I'll do everything I can to make it happen.

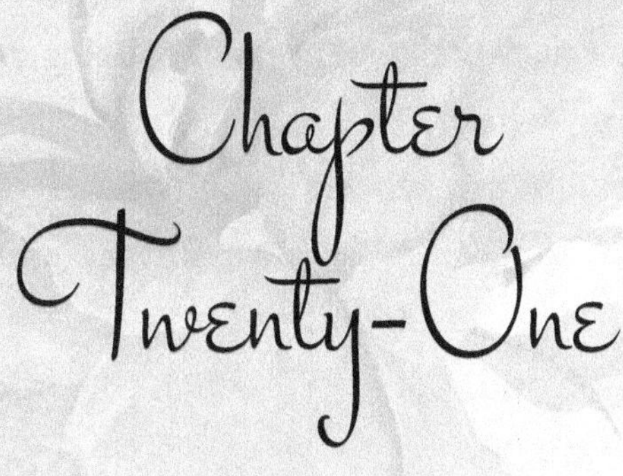

Madison

"It was nice of Mel to let us use his kitchen," I say.

We'd gotten caught up in our tree decorating activities and by the time we got back to the diner, Mel was closing up.

"Yes. It was. Even if all he left us with was a frozen pizza."

"I happen to have a fondness for frozen pizza," I say.

"Okay. Let me see if I can follow directions here," He says as he reads the back of the pizza box.

"I think you just sort of throw it in there."

He looks up. "Wait a minute. The girl who has a spreadsheet outlining her life doesn't follow cooking directions?"

"I pick my battles," I say. "Actually I do read boxes. That's how I know you just throw it in there."

"Okay," he says. "But since we only have one pizza, I'm just going to follow the directions."

I wince. "Good point. We might be rationing food before we know it."

"It's not going to come to that," he says with certainty, keeping his gaze on the back of the pizza box.

"You sound rather sure of that."

"I'm manifesting."

"How does that work exactly?" I take two bottles of water from the refrigerator and set them on the our table.

The shades are drawn and the doors are locked, so we have the diner to ourselves.

Scout ate a bowl of dog food, then curled up in front of the door and went to sleep.

"I wish I knew," he says, finally sliding the pizza into the oven. "I think I could have achieved a lot more."

"I know, right. What do you think Jack and Hannah are doing right now?" I ask.

"Probably watching a movie with Trenton and Olivia."

"Are Trenton and Olivia really a thing?"

"I think they are."

"Don't we think that's odd?"

"I don't think I'm going to answer that right now," he says.

Smiling to myself, I wander back to the kitchen. "He's got a sound system in here."

"Really? I didn't know that."

"You've never been back here in the kitchen, have you?"

"Not even once. How does that thing work?"

"I don't know." I press a button and music starts filling the diner. "I guess it just works like that."

"Eighties music. Mel has good taste."

I smile. "I never would have thought it."

When a familiar slow song starts playing, Lucas holds out a hand. "Care to dance?" he asks.

"Here?"

"Why not?"

"Okay." I put a hand in his and he pulls me close.

He's taller than me. I hadn't quite realized how much. The top of my head reaches just beneath his chin.

"This might be the best Christmas I've ever had," he says.

I look up, my gaze meeting his. "I don't know what to think about that."

I don't know what to think, because I know it's the best Christmas I've ever had.

He suddenly twirls me around and brings me back against him.

"You're good at this," I say. "Did you learn to dance in your wild football days?"

"Something like that."

"I can't tell if that's a yes or a no," I say.

"None of that matters now," he says, looking into my eyes.

"It made you who you are," I say, feeling slightly breathless.

"True. But all that matters is right here. Right now."

The timer on the oven goes off, alerting us that our pizza might be ready.

"I have to get that," he says.

"I know."

He kisses me on the forehead and leaves me to pull our frozen pizza out of the oven.

I drop into the nearest chair and wonder just how much trouble I'm getting myself into.

By such a quirk of chance I ended up here.

A place I wasn't supposed to be with a man who wasn't supposed to be here either.

And we certainly weren't supposed to be together. And yet... And yet we work.

We're good together.

Maybe it's just the clean mountain air.

Or maybe it's the prospect of being stuck here forever in the little town of Luchara.

Whatever it is, I don't quite know what to make of the way I feel about him.

I like him.

And I'm pretty sure I would have liked him no matter where we met.

I just don't know if we would have gotten the chance to know each other if we'd met under different circumstances.

Chapter Twenty-Two

Lucas

AFTER OUR PIZZA and some ice cream we find in Mel's freezer, we put on our coats and walk away from town toward the cabin.

"It's going to snow again," I say, looking up.

"How do you know?" Madison asks, following my gaze.

"The stars. On a clear night, the stars up here are bright and seem impossibly close. But when there are snow clouds, we can only see a few of the stars shining through."

"So you think they're snow clouds?"

"I just feels like snow. Growing up here in the mountains, you start to get a feel for these things."

"I hope it does snow," she says. "It's supposed to snow on Christmas."

"Says the girl from Houston who's never seen real snow."

"Snow at Christmas is on my ideal Christmas list. For someday."

"You might just get your wish this year," I say. If I could make it snow tomorrow, I would do it.

I turn on the flashlight as we leave town with its old-fashioned lamp posts, heading down the trail toward the cabin. A wolf howls somewhere in the distance and a second later, another one not too far away answers with a howl of its own.

Sensing Madison's hesitation, I take her hand.

"We'll be home in a few minutes," I say.

"Not soon enough," she says.

"Sleepy?"

"A little."

I know she is. I can see it in her eyes.

"But," she says. "We have gifts to wrap tomorrow."

"Yes. We do." The weight of the bags with the gifts we'd bought is heavy in my left hand. The one roll of wrapping paper we'd found at the store sticks out of the top of the bag. We each bought some gifts the other one doesn't know about.

It reminds me of when I was a kid and the whole family would pile into the car and drive into Boulder on Christmas Eve. We'd go to the mall and buy last minute gifts for everyone. There had been a lot of slipping around getting surprise gifts for everyone. Nothing big. Just little fun things. Like a box of cookies for Grandma and a fishing lure for Grandpa.

I had fond memories of being part of a big family. We'd been close then and I miss it. And even though we're not close in the same way anymore, I'm going to miss being with my family tomorrow at Christmas.

Reaching the cabin, I unlock the door. Scout races in first, claiming his place in front of the fireplace.

I flip on the lights, chasing away the worst of the darkness and reluctantly let go of Madison's hand.

"I'll take my shopping bag," she says. "Wouldn't want you to accidentally peek inside and ruin your surprise."

"Same here," I say, taking my own bag and stashing it on the kitchen counter to sort through and wrap everything up tomorrow.

It's a nice reminder that even though I'm not with my family, I'm with Madison and she's a different kind of family.

She's the person I can see myself starting a family of my own with.

"I'm going to get ready for bed," she says, heading into the bedroom.

"Take your time," I say.

I open a can of dog food for Scout and set it out for him. As he happily gobbles it up, I change out the water in his bowl.

It feels colder tonight.

I go outside and bring in an armload of wood. Get a fire going in the fireplace.

With that done, I pull a bottle of pinot noir out of my shopping bag. I was going to bring it out tomorrow, but tonight seems like a good time to open it.

Uncorking it, I pour some wine into two plastic wine glasses I'd borrowed from Mel and wait for Madison to come out.

We have a nice romantic fire in the fireplace. Some good wine. It's a nice way to end the evening.

And it really is the turning out to be the best Christmas I've ever had.

Chapter Twenty-Three

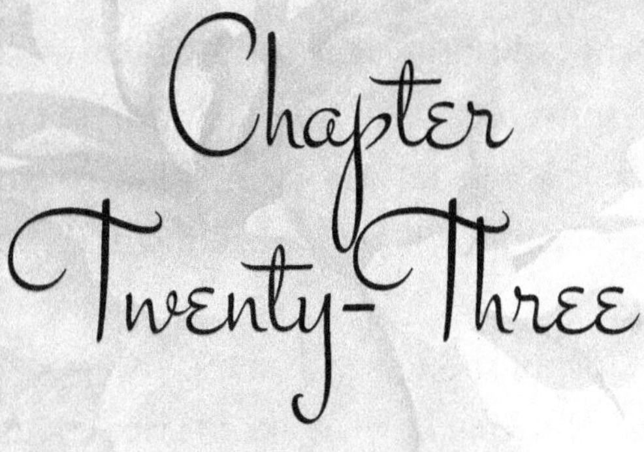

Madison

Wearing my pajamas, my face freshly washed, and my hair brushed, I walk out into the living room to find Lucas waiting for me.

"I was going to save this for tomorrow," he says, handing me a glass of wine, but then I realized we might as well have some tonight, too."

"Our Eve of Christmas Eve celebration," I say.

"Exactly."

"To uncertain times," he says, tapping his glass gently to mine.

I sit on my pallet and take a sip of the wine. It's deep with a slight nutty flavor. This is one of those times when I wish I'd taken the time to study wines. Maybe when I revise my spreadsheet, and I will be overhauling it, I'll add learning about wines on there.

"Penny for your thoughts," he says.

"I was just thinking how I'd like to learn about wines."

"Me too," he says. "Maybe that's something we can do together. When we get out of here."

"Okay," I say, forcing myself not to think about just how impossible that is with him living here in the mountains and me living in Houston.

It makes me think more about my life revisions. Not that I have to make those kinds of changes right now. If I had my phone, I'd take some notes. Start organizing my ideas.

Lucas sits on his pallet and Scout stands up, shakes, and goes to sit next to him, putting his head in his lap.

"Oh," Lucas says. "So you've decided to do some sucking up."

"He loves you," I say.

"I know." He scratches his dog's ears. "And I know how hard it is to not be enamored by a pretty girl."

I raise an eyebrow, but don't say anything.

Somewhere outside, a wolf howls, sending an involuntary chill down my spine. I'm glad we're safely inside the warm cabin away from any wildlife dangers.

"We should call Hannah and Jack tomorrow," I say. "Wish them a happy wedding."

"We will. What would you be doing if you weren't here? If you were in Houston?"

"Usually just spending some time with my family. But not this year. This year my parents are on a cruise and my brother is with his girlfriend."

"Oh. I'm sorry."

"No. It's okay." I take a sip of wine and pull one of the blankets over my feet. "My family never really got into Christmas traditions."

"I see. That's why you have an extensive list of things to do on an ideal Christmas."

"I suppose it is. I never really put that together." I study the wine in my glass as it reflects the light from the fire.

"Psychology degree finally came in handy after all these years."

Turning, I look over at Lucas from beneath my lashes. The overhead light is out and I can only see him in the shadows from the firelight. He's stretched out on his own blankets, looking all the world like a man relaxed without a care in the world.

He's stranded here with me, a stranger, for Christmas, missing Christmas with his family and his brother's wedding, and he doesn't seem to be the least bit bothered by it.

"Have you ever thought about going back and getting your masters in psychology?"

"Nah," he says, swirling the wine in his glass.

"Why not? Most people who get advanced degrees in psychology are older."

"How do you know that?" he asks.

"I'm like a sponge," I say. "And I used to be a dog walker for educated, rich people. I listen."

"Maybe you should go back for your masters."

"I don't think so." I look into the flames again. One of the logs fall, sending sparks up the chimney. "I'm ready to do something to make money."

"What's that going to be?" he asks.

"I don't know yet. The pet adoption thing isn't it. I need something else."

"You need to think bigger," he says.

"Yes! Bigger. I just don't know what it is yet."

"You'll figure it out," he says.

"I know. I've learned that if I don't force it, it'll come to me."

"It will."

Chapter Twenty-Four

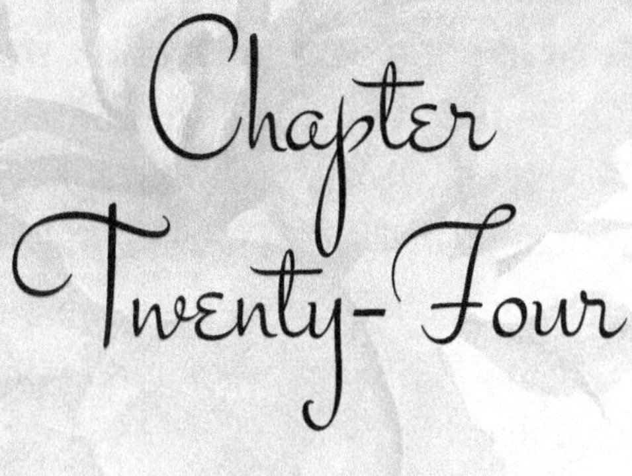

Lucas

SITTING in front of a cozy fire on a cold winter's night with a pretty girl, my dog sleeping next to me, life can't get any better.

We have a huge Christmas tree standing in one corner of the room, decorated with paper chains and popcorn strung on a fishing line and at the very top is a star Madison made out of red and white construction paper. I can imagine just how festive the tree would be if it had lights on it, but even without lights it has an undeniable charm.

She looks relaxed over there on her little pile of blankets, but I can sense the tension beneath the veneer.

She's gotten herself worried about how we're going to get out of here and it's a valid concern. The road is completely destroyed. It can take months to build a road on the side of the mountain like the one that got washed away.

I also sense something deeper going on with her, but that's just a hunch. I get the impression that she's searching for a new direction in life.

I have some ideas about that, but I don't think she's ready to hear them yet. So I keep them to myself.

"What's one of your favorite Christmas memories?" I ask her.

"Oh." She pushes her hair back off her face. "Like I said, we didn't have a lot of traditions."

"Surely you have some fond memories."

"My brother and I used to go outside and light sparklers on Christmas Eve."

"Sparklers. Those are fun."

"We were young. So yeah. And we had this dog. Spot. Spot was so funny. We'd wrap him a little gift and put it under the tree. Not in a box or anything. Just a chew toy. Like a stuffed frog. It could sit there for days and he wouldn't touch it. Then when we started opening presents, he'd go under the tree, get his present and tear off the paper."

"Now you're just making this up."

"Not even a little."

"That's a good memory."

"Yeah. What about you? What's one of your favorite Christmas memories?"

"One year my mom got mad at us. Having three boys, it's understandable. But that year she decided that instead of having Christmas at home doing the normal things, we'd all go into Boulder and spend the day volunteering at the homeless shelter."

"Seriously?"

"Seriously. It was one of the most satisfying Christmases I ever had."

"You liked helping people."

"I did. I felt like I made a difference."

"You only did it that one time?"

"It never came up again. I guess she was satisfied with whatever she was trying to teach us that year. I'd do it again though."

"But you enjoy being with your family."

"As crazy as they are, yes. I've never missed spending a Christmas with them."

"Maybe we'll have a Christmas miracle and you can make it this year."

"It would take a miracle," I say. "But it's okay. I'm content to spend Christmas right here. With you."

She smiles a little and looks away.

Maybe she doesn't believe me or maybe she's thinking practically. About how she lives in Houston and I live in Alpine Falls.

What she doesn't realize is that there's more than one kind of Christmas miracle.

They come in all shapes and sizes.

And she just might need to be open to a miracle of her own.

Chapter Twenty-Five

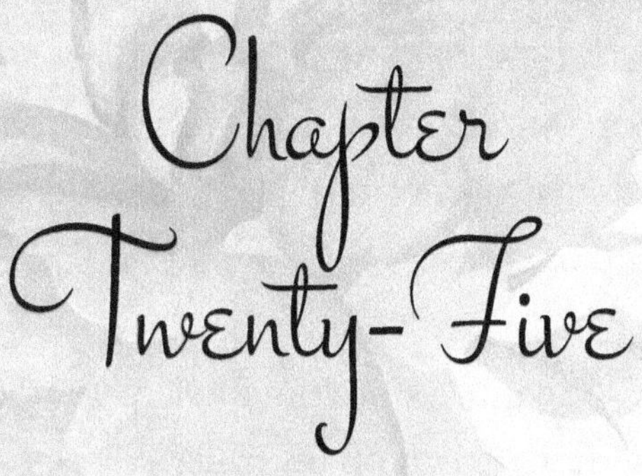

Madison

I WAKE to the sound of Christmas music.

Deciding I must be dreaming, I turn over and pull the blanket over my face.

But then I smell the scent of bacon and eggs.

And coffee.

It's enough to wake me up the rest of the way.

"Good morning, Sunshine," Lucas says.

I sit up and look at him. "Good morning. You've got food. And coffee."

"I woke up early so I went into town and got us breakfast to go. Thought you might like Christmas Eve breakfast in bed."

"I've never had Christmas Eve breakfast in bed."

"I figured if it wasn't on the list it should be." He hands me a to-go cup of coffee.

"It is now," I say, with a smile.

He hands me a takeout container of food and, holding one for himself, sits down on his pallet.

"You seem happy today," I say, opening the lid to find a full meal of bacon, eggs, and two pieces of toast.

"It's Christmas Eve. The most magical day of the year."

"More so than Christmas Day?"

"I think so. When Christmas Day gets here, the magic is winding down."

"I tend to agree with you," I say. "You must have been up for awhile. You built a fire. You walked into town." I glance back at the tree. There are gifts wrapped in festive red and some wrapped in plain brown paper I didn't know we had. "You wrapped your presents."

"I did," he says, grinning. "And you slept through it all."

"I'm sort of a heavy sleeper," I say.

"It's a good trait to have. What do you want to do today?"

"Well. I need to wrap my gifts."

"That won't take long."

"It always takes longer than it should."

"I can help you."

I point my fork at him. "Nice try, big guy."

He grins.

"Considering that they're all for you."

"Aw. You shouldn't have."

"Wait," I say. "Are all those presents under the tree for Scout?"

"One of them. No. Two of them."

"The rest are mine?"

"Who else would they be for?"

I shrug. "I don't know. Maybe you bought presents for Mel and the other merchants in town."

"No. I would consult with you if I did that."

I hide my surprise behind my coffee cup. He would consult with me?

That's new. That's not something I expected him to say.

"This is really good," I say.

"It's the crisp—"

"mountain air." I finish the sentence for him.

Grinning, he looks at me again.

"I have an idea," he says.

"Okay. I like ideas."

"You've got wedding clothes in your car, right?"

"Right."

"Since it's Christmas Eve, why don't we wear our nice clothes? You know. Just to make it special."

"Oh." I give him a little nod. "I like that idea."

"Good. Me too."

"You have your wedding clothes here?"

"Oddly enough. Yes. Don't ask."

"Okay. I won't ask. I'm going to take a shower first though and wrap my gifts."

"Perfect. I saved you some wrapping paper."

I wonder what's gotten into Lucas. Maybe he just woke up with Christmas spirit and I happen to be the lucky recipient of it all.

Not complaining. Not even a little bit.

Chapter Twenty-Six

Lucas

By mid-morning on Christmas Eve, all our gifts are wrapped and under the tree. Scout doesn't go near them. I wonder if dogs somehow have a weird understanding of wrapped Christmas gifts because I know for a fact that there are doggy treats under there that he can smell.

I bring Madison's suitcase in and she disappears into the bedroom. Since I'm already wearing my tux which I'd picked up in Boulder on my way here—some things are just fortuitous that way—I busy myself with some house plan drawings.

I've got my plans for this cabin finished up, so I entertain myself with some rough plans for a house I've been thinking about building for myself.

Maybe I should have gotten that degree in architecture. I could go back, still, and do it. But my brother, Trenton, can help me with any details and finishing touches after I get through playing. I'll probably never even do anything with all the house plans I've sketched out. It's just something I enjoy doing.

After what seems like forever, the bedroom door opens and Madison steps out.

She looks absolutely stunning and I'm speechless.

Her dress is in a dark crimson color, for Christmas, the color of a cardinal. I remember Hannah telling Olivia that her colors were inspired by a Christmas cardinal she'd seen perched on a window when she first got to our house, but I hadn't realized just how stunning the color would be in an evening gown on the prettiest girl I've ever seen.

She did something with her hair, too. It's straight with little curls at the ends. And she's wearing makeup. Her lashes are long and dark. Her eyelids sparkly and her lips glossy.

I just sit there, staring at her.

"Is this okay?" she asks, jarring me out of my daze.

"You're stunning," I say.

And now I have the answer to the question I'd been asking myself.

I'd asked myself if I would have noticed her at the wedding if we hadn't met like we had.

The answer is an absolutely hell yes.

Anyone would notice Madison and I can't look away.

"You look nice, too," she says. "Do you have your phone? Let's take a photo in front of our tree."

Shoving my paper aside, I pull out my phone and meet her in front of our Christmas tree.

I put my arm around her and we lean together, smiling for the camera.

I lower the camera, but neither one of us moves.

Turning slightly, keeping my arm around her, I look into her lovely green eyes.

We don't need lights on the Christmas tree.

We don't need music.

We have everything we need.

I lower my head and kiss her.

She closes her eyes and neither one of us moves as we stand there, our lips pressed together.

This. This is the meaning of life.

Scout stands up and barks once, breaking the moment.

"I think Scout wants to go outside," I say.

"It's time for us to go to lunch anyway."

"I guess it is."

I look down and grin. "I see you're wearing my boots with that dress."

"What can I say? I'm a practical girl."

"I can get behind that."

"Let's get our coats on and go see what Mel's cooking."

Scout barks again and dances around in a little circle.

"Scout agrees with that idea," she says.

"Scout agrees with just about anything."

Except kissing. Unfortunately, he doesn't seem to be too tolerant of kissing.

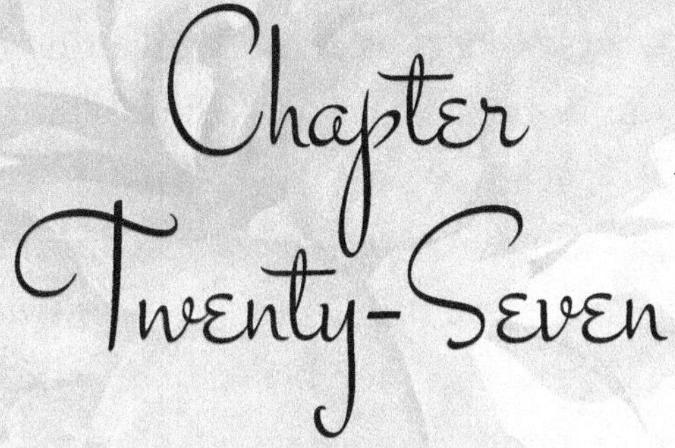

Chapter Twenty-Seven

Madison

It should feel a little odd, wearing the dress I was going to wear to Hannah's wedding to lunch at the Luchara diner, especially since we have to walk along a curvy mountain trail to get there.

It's so peacefully quiet. Nothing but the sound of the wind whispering through the trees. The steady roar of the river, water rushing past us as we walk along the bank for a time. Little patches of snow, protected from the sun, beneath the trees. The scent of wood smoke from the various fireplaces, including ours.

And yet, walking alongside Lucas, wearing his tux, my hand in his, his dog trotting along beside us, it doesn't seem strange at all.

Instead of feeling strange, it feels like Christmas and that makes it okay. With the magic of Christmas swirling in the air, it doesn't seem the least bit strange at all. Not even wearing Lucas's boots that are several sizes too big for me beneath my evening gown.

The diner is packed and Mel seems happier than I've seen him in the time I've spent here. The guests, locals and tourists alike, aren't even talking about the avalanche or wondering how we're all going to get out of here.

It's like everyone made a tacit agreement to take a break from talking about it, even if only for just one day.

After lunch, walking back to the cabin, the sun shining, Scout runs through the trees and comes out somewhere behind us only to race past us.

"He's such a funny dog," I say.

"Yeah. I like him."

"He's a good fit for you," I say.

"Is there some hidden meaning there?" he asks.

"I don't know what you mean," I say, smiling over at him.

Walking among the blue spruce trees, holding hands with Lucas feels right.

Impossibly impractical, but at the same time right.

"Should we open our presents tonight?" he asks. "Or tomorrow?"

"Both," I say. "Some tonight. But save some for in the morning."

"Okay. I like that plan."

I slow down as a sound registers.

"What is it?" Lucas asks, slowing down, too.

"Do you hear that?" I ask.

"The helicopter?"

"Yes. That's what it is." It sounds so strange out here in the quiet wilderness. I feel like I haven't heard a car motor or anything modern in forever. "Flying over checking things out?"

"Could be," he says, looking up.

I follow his gaze until I see the helicopter flying this way.

"It's landing." I say, not sure if I'm asking or telling.

But it is landing. Up ahead near the cabin.

"Why is it landing?" I ask.

"Let's go see," he says, squeezing my hand.

By the time we reach the cabin, the helicopter's motor is turned off, leaving just its faint echo lingering in the air.

We round a bend in the trail and there's the helicopter sitting in a clearing that looks all the world like it was make for it, not far from my car and his truck.

Then I see Hannah.

Hannah?

And Olivia. And Jack and another man who must be Trenton.

"They're here?" I ask Lucas.

Lucas is grinning.

"Looks like it," he says.

"You knew they were coming." Not waiting for an answer, I pull my hand free and rush forward to hug my two friends.

"What are you doing here?" I ask.

"We came to get you," Hannah says. "I couldn't get married without you at the wedding. And your dress, Madison. It's beautiful."

"You picked it out."

"I know, but I didn't expect it to look so great."

I glance at my watch. "Your wedding."

"Plenty of time," Olivia says. "Alpine Falls is like a ten minute flight from here."

I look at Jack. "Wait. Jack flies helicopters?"

"Did I not mention that?" Hannah asks innocently. "Jack does so much. It's hard to keep up."

"We've got to get your phone replaced," Olivia says.

Lucas walks up to his brothers.

"Looks like you've got some explaining to do," Jack says.

"Been keeping secrets," Trenton says, nodding toward the stack of wood.

"I'll tell you all about it," Lucas says. "But we've got a wedding to get to."

"Do we have room for some luggage and things?" I ask.

"Plenty of room," Jack says. "What needs to go?"

"I need a few minutes to pack up," I say, heading toward the cabin.

"We'll help you," Olivia says. "Come on, Hannah."

"We've got to get Hannah dressed," I say.

"All in due time," Olivia says.

They follow me into the cabin.

"Lucas has a Christmas tree," Hannah says with obvious surprise.

"Actually we do. We picked it out and decorated it ourselves. Hold on a minute."

I walk back to the door. "Lucas? We're taking our gifts, right?"

"Of course," he says. "I'll bag them up. Don't worry. Just get packed up. We're getting out of here."

"Right." I look over at the tree and feel a wave of sadness wash over me.

I'd gotten so wrapped up in spending Christmas with Lucas that even seeing my friends, even getting to attend Hannah's wedding, even getting out of Luchara doesn't make up for not getting to spend Christmas with Lucas.

I square my shoulders and pull myself up by my innate practicality.

Getting out of here is a good thing.

And we've got a wedding in just hours.

Besides. It's okay because Lucas will be there, too.

Chapter Twenty-Eight

Lucas

It had taken everything I had to not tell Madison my secret.

I talked to Jack this morning and we made tentative plans for him to fly over and get us. He hadn't been able to guarantee that it would be today though. Since Jack doesn't own a helicopter, it had taken some work for him to find one that he could borrow. Apparently all the pilots with helicopters that he could call upon were using them until now.

Hannah had insisted that they all come, wedding or no.

I feel a twinge of nostalgia as I pack up the presents beneath our tree. It has been a memorable couple of days to say the least.

Madison and I had created something together. We'd made a good thing out of a bad situation.

I hadn't been exaggerating when I'd said it was the best Christmas I'd ever had.

But just because we're relocating doesn't mean that will change. We're taking the Christmas we created with us.

It'll be good to be with my family, especially since Madison will be there, too.

Having Madison spend Christmas with my family only adds to the perfectness of this year's Christmas, even if it does mean that we have to leave our little haven.

"This is interesting," Trenton says, lifting one of the paper chains.

"Madison and I made those," I say with obvious pride. "We strung the popcorn, too. With fishing line."

Jack and Trenton exchange a look.

"You should get stranded with a pretty girl more often," Jack says. "It suits you."

"Well," I say, reaching under the tree and pulling out gifts. "We thought we were going to be spending Christmas here."

"Not on my watch," Jack says. "If I can help it."

I stand up and put a hand on Jack's shoulder. "You're a good brother." No point in telling him that I was perfectly content to be stranded here with Madison.

"Can I make a suggestion?" Trenton asks.

"Sure."

"While the girls are packing up, we can undecorate this tree. Then use the decorations to put on a tree in your apartment over the barn."

I look blankly at him.

"It would be a nice surprise for Madison," he says. "Don't know when you'll get back up here."

"It's not a bad idea," I say. It's actually a very good idea. "But I'll take them off if you'll pack up my power tools from the truck. Assuming you have room for them."

"We have room," Jack says. "Come on Trenton, let's give Lucas a minute."

"I don't need a minute," I say in a weak protest as they walk off. But looking at the tree, I decide maybe I do.

Madison and I invested a lot in this tree and taking the decorations with us is a good idea. A very good idea. And I think Madison will like it.

If I had time, which I don't, I'd get her something nice for Christmas. Instead, all I have are these little gifts from the General Store.

But maybe it really is the thought that counts.

If it's the thought that counts, then I'm giving her my heart.

Chapter Twenty-Nine

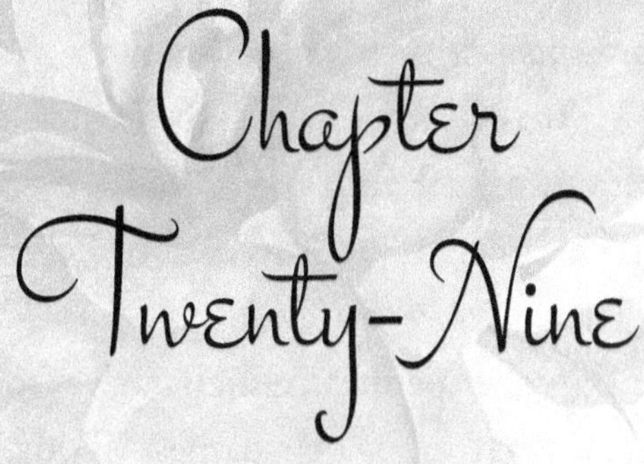

Madison

FLYING AWAY from Luchara in the helicopter, my hand firmly in Lucas's, Scout sitting between us, I watch the little cabin, then the little town, then the destroyed road, vanish below.

I'm happy to be leaving. I really am.

If it hadn't been for Lucas being there, I'm not sure I could have stood it. I'd probably have gone into a full blown panic.

As it is, having him next to me now makes leaving here tolerable.

"We'll come back and visit," he says.

"Maybe." I frown out the window, then look back at him. "What about my car and your truck?"

"Jack said he can get them lifted out by helicopter."

"Oh." I'll have to worry about the cost of that later. "What about the other people in Luchara?"

"The guys... what were their names? Teddy and Ralph? They're working on that."

"But we have inside help."

"Family comes in handy at times," he says.

"As does found family," I say and he squeezes my hand.

"You'll always have a place with us," he says. "No matter what happens."

"Thank you," I say, finding it a rather odd thing for him to say. I can't help looking for his true meaning behind the words. Maybe it's because I'm Hannah's friend and she's marrying his brother.

It just seems like an odd thing for him to say after kissing me. Maybe that kiss had simply been him getting swept up in the moment.

"We're here," he says just as the helicopter starts its descent.

I hold onto his hand in response to the sudden change in direction.

We land behind his parents' house, proving that there are most definitely benefits to a helicopter over even a small private airplane that requires a runway.

We're unloaded in no time and I'm set up in a room with Olivia.

There's no time to dally, though, because we have to turn Hannah into a bride befitting a wedding, even if it is a small wedding.

It takes Olivia five minutes to change into her dress that matches mine perfectly and we're off to Hannah's room. She's already had a shower and is working on drying her hair.

When did my friends get so fast at getting ready? Or maybe I slowed down.

Either way, the three of us go into a flurry of activity, getting Hannah into her wedding gown, doing her hair and makeup.

"What's Lucas like?" Hannah asks as Olivia smears eyeshadow on her lids.

"What do you mean?" I ask, turning on the hair straightener. It seems like such an odd question coming from someone who is practically related to Lucas.

"Just curious," she says. "We don't get to spend much time with him so I don't really know him. You've probably spent more time with him in two days than I have in fifteen years."

"Oh. Well. That's sad." I pick up a brush and run it through my own hair. "He's a very nice guy. A gentleman. Kind. And thoughtful."

"He seems that way," Olivia says. "Likeable."

"Yes. He's likeable."

"Did he mention why he doesn't come around the family much? He lives on the property, you know. He has an apartment over the barn and he's either there taking care of the horses or off somewhere."

Because he doesn't feel appreciated. But it's not my place to tell anyone that. Not even my closest friends. Especially not the friend who's about to marry his brother.

"He's private, I guess. And just does his own thing."

"What's the deal with the cabin?" Olivia asks. "It's obviously under construction. Trenton said he had tools in his truck. I didn't know Lucas did that kind of work."

"I don't know," I say. "All I know is he was nice enough to let me stay there when there weren't any rooms in town."

Olivia clucks her tongue and gets to work on Hannah's eyelashes. "It looked cozy to me."

"It was cozy," I say. "It snowed and we were warm. I'm going downstairs to get us some water."

Turning on my heels, the high heels I'm wearing now, I leave them there. Let them speculate. I don't care.

I know what it's like to be a private person. I've always been the most private person I know.

I hadn't really noticed coming in, but I stop at the bottom of the stairs and admire the deep red poinsettias on every surface. On the little table behind the sectional. On the coffee table. On the mantle.

I wander to the fireplace and find Cupcake, Olivia's little Yorkshire terrier with an adorable caramel colored head and a white body sitting in front of the fire, mesmerized by the flames. It's thanks to her unusual coloring that Olivia gave up on finding someone willing to adopt Cupcake and kept her for her own dog.

I sit down on the ledge next to her.

"Hey Cupcake. You like the fire?" I rub her head, warm from the fire. "Do you like the warmth or the flames?"

Cupcake doesn't answer.

"Both. Me too. Where did the guys get off to? It looks like everything is just about ready for your Aunt Hannah's wedding."

Cupcake barks once.

"Do you want to go outside?"

Cupcake barks again and hops off the ledge, running toward the back door.

"I guess that means yes."

Following her to where she waits at the back door, I find her leash and clip it onto her harness.

With Cupcake leading the way, we step outside onto the back deck and walk down the stairs to the backyard.

Holding the leash with one hand, I hold the banister with the other as I navigate the stairs with high heels I'm not accustomed to wearing. I was much more comfortable wearing Lucas's hiking boots even if they were too big for me.

While Cupcake searches for the perfect spot to do her business, I see the three guys heading my way as they come out of the trees by way of a dirt trail that reminds me of the walkway from the cabin to the diner in Luchara.

"There she is," Jack says.

"And neither one of them is wearing a coat," Trenton says.

I'm shivering and I hadn't even realized it. Cupcake is shivering, too.

"Cupcake has a coat?"

"Absolutely," Trenton says.

"Cupcake," I say sternly. "You didn't tell me you were supposed to wear a coat."

Smiling, Lucas removes his own coat and drapes it over my shoulders.

"Thank you," I say, looking into his blue eyes.

"You're welcome." He takes Cupcake's leash from me and hands her over to Trenton. "Her daddy is a bit overprotective."

"I am not." But he takes her leash and leads her back toward the house.

"Sorry," I say. "I just needed some fresh air and Cupcake needed to come outside."

"It's okay. It takes a minute to get used to needing a coat when you walk outside even for a few minutes."

"I guess it does. It's almost time for the wedding. Everything okay?"

"Yeah. We just had something we had to take care of before Jack jets off on his honeymoon."

"They're flying?"

"Of course. While he has the helicopter, he's taking Hannah somewhere."

"Where are they going?"

"I don't know. He won't tell me."

"A surprise honeymoon. I wonder what Hannah thinks about that."

"I think Hannah probably has a good idea. She would have to. To pack."

"True."

"So. The girls ran you off?"

"No." I sigh. "They kept asking too many questions." I turn sideways as the wind blows hair into my face.

"What kind of questions?"

"They wanted to know about you and the cabin. It wasn't my business to tell them. So I didn't."

He smooths the hair off my face. "I appreciate your loyalty, but I just told Jack and Trenton what I was doing there. So you don't have to keep my secrets anymore."

"Well. Now you tell me."

He grins. "I have something I want to show you. After the wedding."

"After the wedding? Trying to keep me in suspense?"

"Absolutely. It's a Christmas Eve surprise."

"Then it must be good," I say.

"I think you'll like it. Ready to go back inside now? Get those two married off."

"Sure."

"By the way," he says. "Just between you and me. I think Trenton and Olivia are going to be getting married next."

"You really think so?" I ask, as he takes my hand and we walk together up the stairs leading to the back deck.

"I really do."

"Don't you think that's a little odd? Your brother getting married to your other brother's wife's friend? Never mind. It's too complicated."

"I don't happen to think it's strange at all. I think it's quite efficient."

"Efficient."

He opens the door and we walk into the warmth of the house.

"You have to admit the efficiency is a bonus." He takes his coat off my shoulders and hangs it up. "Looks like everyone is here and the wedding is about to start."

"I'm not sure they were going to wait for us," I say.

"Welcome to my world."

"I'm beginning to understand a little better what you were talking about," I say as we take our places.

Chapter Thirty

Lucas

THE WEDDING WAS as it should have been. Simple and
sweet.

My brother, Jack, and Hannah were first married over
ten years ago. Shortly after the wedding, something
happened and there was a divorce. Supposedly a divorce.

Hannah spent ten years believing they were divorced,
but Jack knew they were still married. He knew because he
never signed the papers.

All that time, he remained faithful to Hannah.

Since she didn't know she was still married, she dated
others. In fact, she was engaged to someone else when she
showed up in Alpine Falls seeking a copy of divorce papers

that didn't exist when she learned she was still married to Jack.

The rest is history. They decided to renew their vows for a fresh start.

Smart idea considering all the water that flowed under that bridge.

Hannah is a beautiful bride. There's no denying that. But Madison is the girl I can't take my eyes off of.

During the ceremony, she looks in my direction and our gazes lock. Her cheeks flush prettily. Fate. Kismet. Whatever label someone chooses, it feels to me like it's meant to be.

Trenton and Olivia will be married next. Now all I have to do is convince Madison to stay here. We can built a house of our own. I don't even care where we live. If she wants to live in Houston, I can do that, too, even though I'd rather stay around here.

Small wedding. Just family. So the reception consists of our dad opening bottles of champagne and everyone getting a glass.

It's obvious that Jack and Hannah are ready to get out of here.

"We have to get going before it gets dark," Jack says.

"You know you can wait until morning to leave," Dad says.

"We know," Jack pulls Hannah close. "But we have reservations."

"Go," Mother says. "Don't be trying to fly that chopper at night.

"Take good care of Bandit," Hannah says, picking up her cat and holding him close against her.

"You know we'll take care of him like he's ours," Olivia says.

"He'll be fine." Madison leans in and gives Hannah a hug. "Enjoy yourself."

We follow them outside and watch as they board the helicopter.

I figure they've got about one good hour of flying before the sun dips below the horizon. That tells me they aren't going far. They don't have to go far to feel like a world away from here. I know that from experience.

Standing next to Madison, we watch the helicopter until it's just a speck on the horizon, then we can't see it anymore.

"We're going inside," Olivia says. "You coming?"

"We'll be along in a bit," I say. "Come on," I tell Madison. "I have something to show you."

Suddenly feeling a little bit nervous, I take her hand and lead her down the path toward the barn where I have a little apartment on the second floor.

"Remember I told you I moved in over the barn to help out after my dad's accident?" I ask.

"Sure. I remember. Is that where we're going?"

"Yes. Promise me you won't be judgy."

"When have I been judgy?" she asks, looking over at me.

"You haven't. That's why you get to see my little apartment."

"I'm honored," she says.

Grinning, I take her hand.
"I'll remind you of that," I say.
She just smiles back.

Chapter Thirty-One

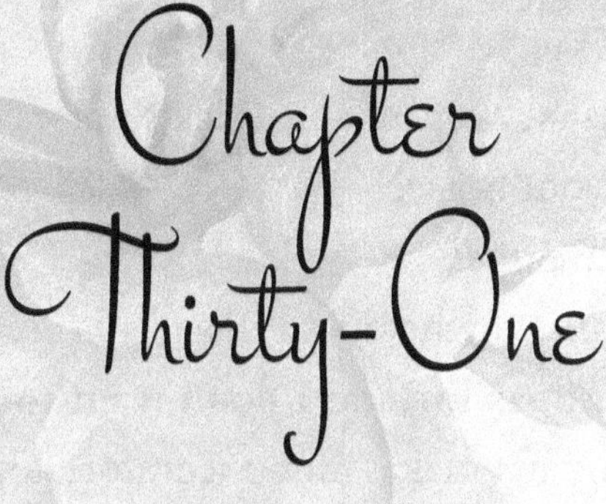

Madison

THE BARN as he called it is more like a stable in my opinion.
On the first floor, there are individual stalls for two dozen
horses.

"Only fifteen of them are filled," he tells me.

"Still. Fifteen horses." Having never been in a barn or a
stable before, I'm a little surprised by the strong scent of hay
and animals. Scout, walking along beside us, seems to know
exactly where he's going.

Pausing, I peak into one of the stalls and see a large dapple gray horse.

"Pretty," I say.

"Yeah. That's Morgan. She's Jack's horse."

"Where's your horse?"

"I don't have one."

I start to ask why he doesn't have a horse, but decide to wait. It's Christmas Eve and I don't want to make him talk about anything that makes him uncomfortable.

"You're welcome to help me feed them later, if you want."

"Sure. But I don't know about the mucking part."

"I won't make you muck the stalls."

"Thank you."

Reaching a door, about halfway through the first floor of the barn, he opens it up and we go upstairs.

I don't know what I expected, but I did not expect this.

The apartment is more like what I would call a loft or maybe a studio apartment and it still smells like freshly cut wood.

It has a medium sized bed. Nothing too small. Nothing too big. Nicely made as I had suspected from the way he kept the bedding folded at the cabin.

There's a love seat and a little television. A desk with a closed notebook computer on it. A stack of what looks like house plans on one side of the desk.

One wall is all windows looking out over the forest with the snow-capped mountains in the distance. It's the opposite direction from the main house, giving it a very secluded feel.

"This view," I say. "Amazing."

"I know. Doesn't get much better."

"Did you build this space yourself?" I ask, running a hand over the small kitchen table for two. Everything is clean and uncluttered.

"I did most of the work, yes."

"You're really quite handy," I say. "I'm glad you showed me this."

"Me too." He stands back on his heels. "But this isn't what I wanted to show you."

"Oh? There's more?"

"Yes." He grins and moves aside a little tri-fold partition between the window and the desk.

Behind the partition is a real Christmas tree, about five-feet tall. A blue spruce like we'd had in the cabin.

And our paper chains and popcorn strings are looped around it. The little star I'd made from construction paper sits at the top of the tree. And our presents are arranged beneath it.

Turning, I look at him, feeling something catching in my chest.

"It's smaller than our tree," he says. "But it's the best I could do on short notice."

"You recreated our tree," I say, stunned and amazed.

"It didn't seem right to just leave it."

"It's perfect," I say and throw my arms around him.

As he kisses me, Scout barks once, then darts beneath the tree and comes back dragging out one of the gifts in his mouth.

"Look at him," I say. "That's what my dog did."

"That's his present," Lucas says. "His treats."

"He knows."

We watch as Scout uses his mouth to tear the paper off the bag of treats.

Once it's unwrapped enough, Scout looks at us expectantly and Lucas opens the bag and hands him a treat.

"We said we'd open something tonight," Lucas says, reaching down and picking up a gift. "Come sit down and open it."

We sit side by side on the loveseat and I unwrap the gift.

"It's a notebook," I say, not sure what to make of it.

"You like to make lists so I thought you might go old-school. Of course, we were at the cabin at the time." He shrugs.

"I do like to make lists," I say. "And I like to write things down by hand. Thank you."

"You're welcome."

Running a hand along the plain black cover of the notebook, I ask. "Is there anything in particular you were thinking I might want to write down?"

"Yes," he says with a little smile. "As a matter of fact, there is."

"What would that be?" I look into his smiling blue eyes, my heart swelling with happiness.

"I want you to stay," he says.

"Stay? What do you mean?" I have butterflies in my stomach. If he means what I think he means...

"Here. In Alpine Falls. Here." He sweeps a hand back in the direction of the main house. "In the house. With me."

I flip through the blank pages of the notebook. "How long are you thinking I should stay here?"

Scout barks once and jumps onto the sofa, putting his head in my lap.

"Long enough to fill that notebook and a million more like it." Lucas takes my hands. "I want you to stay forever."

I swallow the lump in my throat, but it doesn't go away. "That would take figuring out some details, wouldn't it?"

He taps the notebook. "Hence the notebook."

Biting my lip, I smile. "Hence the notebook. So... I'll live with your parents while you live here?"

"Until we figure things out," he says. "Trenton and Olivia will be getting married next."

I raise an eyebrow, but don't say anything.

"That would give me plenty of time to court you properly."

"You think I need courting?" I ask, unable to resist the smile spreading across my lips.

"A gentleman always courts the woman he plans to marry."

"I see."

Scout licks my hand.

"Scout wants you to stay, too," Lucas says.

"Well. With two handsome boys asking me to stay, how can I resist?"

"Does that mean you'll stay?"

"I have details to work out, but yes. I'll stay."

He leans over and kisses me.

"The best Christmas ever," he whispers against my lips.

"The best," I say.

Epilogue

Madison

One Year Later

"No peeking!" Lucas says.

Holding onto his hand like a lifeline, I keep my other hand over my eyes.

"I'm lost already. Even if I see where I'm going, I won't know where I am."

"You'll ruin the effect," he says. "We're almost there."

I'm wearing my not-quite-broken-in trail boots and a heavy wool coat that's quite suitable for snowy weather.

We've been walking for what I guage to be about fifteen

minutes, give or take, so we're not too far from their house. Our house. My house.

We've followed the river most of the way, too, so I could find my way home if I had to.

"Is it snowing?" I ask. "It's snowing, isn't it? On Christmas Eve."

"Yes," Lucas says. "It's snowing, but that's not your surprise."

I make a sound that has Scout looking up at me.

"What's that?" Lucas asks.

"I didn't say anything."

He stops. "We're here."

"Finally. Can I look now?"

"Yes. You can look."

I open my eyes and the first thing I see is a delightful snowfall. Little fluffy flakes drifting lightly down all around us, landing on my coat sleeves. My eyelashes.

"What do you think?" Lucas asks.

"The snow is beautiful," I say, mostly because I know that's not what he's asking about.

"Not the snow. The view. The trees. The river. Everything."

Shading my eyes with one gloved hand, I look around. We're standing in what I've learned is called a moraine with the river tumbling along beside us.

And the view is just stunning. The river. The moraine with little winter flowers peeking up through the white layer of snow.

"I don't have words to describe this view," I say.

"It's a view you could look at every day, isn't it?"

"Yes. Actually. It is. Very much so."

"It's ours if we want it."

"What do you mean?" I ask, shifting my gaze to his.

"We can have this piece of land to build a house on. If you want to. If you like it."

"We can live here?"

"Yes."

"It's not far from the house or the stables." I've developed a fondness for horses. "And the river. Perfect for sleeping."

"I've been playing around with some house plans, but I thought we could start from the beginning. Make it ours."

"We can design it from scratch. And make the view work for us. Lots and lots of walls of windows." I put my arms around him. "It's going to be perfect."

"It's going to be ours. So yes. Perfect."

"We'll need lots of extra bedrooms with both Hannah and Olivia expecting. Our nieces and nephews can come visit."

"And they can play with our children."

"Our children?" I ask.

"Yes. Our children. You do want children? Right?"

"Of course I do. We talked about that. With dozens and dozens of dogs and cats for them to play with."

"I thought for minute you were going to say dozens and dozens of children."

"I don't think that's physically possible. How about dozens and dozens of grandchildren?"

"Okay." Lucas puts one arm beneath my knees, picks me up and turns around in a circle. "We'll have dozens and dozens of grandchildren."

I tilt my head back, letting the snow fall on my face.

I'm happy.

I'm never been so very happy.

Sometimes I'm so happy it just hits me like a ton of bricks and I can barely believe just how fortunate I am.

An impulsive road trip with a turn down a random road quite simply led me to my forever home.

The End.

AUTHOR OF OUT OF ASHES
KATHRYN KALEIGH
HE WILL RISK IT ALL TO PROTECT HER
Just
BREATHE
THE GRAVITY OF US SERIES

Just Breathe

PREVIEW

Chapter 1
Audrey
Houston, Texas

I became a widow on a stormy Tuesday evening.

I'd just locked up the art gallery on McKinney Street and pulled out of the parking garage when the sky opened up. Blinding rain hammers the roof of my Toyota Camry, loud and relentless, like the storm had been holding its breath until I left work.

My windshield wipers fight hard, but the downpour blurs everything—the road, the streetlights, the familiar city skyline. Sheets of water pour down the window.

Even through the strong new car scent, I smell the rain. Clean and fresh. Washing away the dust of southern humidity.

Normally, I like the rain. It makes the world feel quieter, softer somehow. But not tonight.

I slow at the intersection, squinting through the blur of headlights and storm. Typical spring in Texas—clear skies one moment, flooded roads the next.

I dread the drive home. Even with a straight shot on Interstate 10, it's still a long drive out to Katy. It's a mystery to me and probably always will be just why Thomas wanted to buy a house out in the suburbs when I worked downtown and he spent most of his time at the airport north of town.

So every day, often even on weekends, I get in my car and head east toward downtown while he gets in his car and heads north toward the airport.

As an airplane pilot, he spends the night away from home at least once a week. In his defense, I guess he thought I would be safer out in the suburbs. But the drive...

I hadn't complained. Not when the three-story house, all stone and glass, with its manicured lawn was so pretty. And new. The new house with its brand new appliances. No one else has ever lived in it before us. Considering it was my first house after living in apartments, I'm pretty happy once I get inside.

The gallery had hosted an event tonight for two very different artists. One of them was known for realistic photographs and the other for abstract watercolors.

Two artists, more different in every way possible,

couldn't have been paired together even if we'd tried. Concurrent hosting is new. Something suggested by the new CEO to increase profits.

My job was easy. My job was to make sure everyone else did their job. The hostess. The caterer. Other than that, I spent most of my time talking to guests.

When the first phone call from a number I don't recognize shows up on my dashboard screen, I let it go to voicemail. After an evening of talking to people, I just want time to decompress. That's how I typically use the drive home. I'd replay the evening. Catalog everything away in my head and make room for a glass of wine and a book.

Thomas is on an overnight trip tonight to Austin, so it's just me. I'm looking forward to getting out of my heels and cocktail dress, grabbing a glass of wine, and curling up on the sofa in front of the fireplace with a romance novel.

Thomas and I usually watch a movie or binge watch some series or another, but when I'm alone, I'm content to just spend the evening quietly reading. My go to evening activity before I met Thomas.

The second time my phone rings, I hit the button and send the caller straight to voicemail. I don't need a distraction from driving right now. Not in this thunderstorm.

As though to support my decision, a flash of lightning splits the sky just as I merge onto the interstate followed by an ear-splitting crash of thunder that makes the air tremble.

The third time my phone rings, I'm nearing the outer loop, still gripping the steering wheel, cringing as every car rushes past, sending an extra spray of water onto the windshield. A quick glance tells me it's the same number calling. A local number.

My family lives in Atlanta, so it's either a wrong number or work. This time of night, just after ten, I'm going with wrong number.

But it could be someone with a problem related to the art gallery and as the manager, I'm responsible. I press the answer button on my steering wheel.

"Hello."

"Ms. Albright?"

"This is Audrey." I didn't take Thomas's last name and it rather annoys me that people always assume that I did.

Not that there's anything wrong with a woman taking her husband's name. I just hadn't. And it seems like people shouldn't make assumptions.

"This is John with the FAA."

"The FAA." My stomach knots. "I think you meant to call Thomas's number."

He's quiet for a moment. "Are you driving?"

"Yes." Thunder crashes again and I grip the steering wheel with both hands. Despite the rain and diminished visibility, cars and big eighteen wheelers fly past me on either side.

I just want to be home.

"I hear the storm," he says. "Can I call you back?"

"Sure. But Thomas isn't available."

"It's okay," he says. "I'll call you back."

"Sure thing," I say and disconnect the line.

How had John from the FAA gotten my phone number and why is he calling Thomas late at night?

It probably has something to do with Thomas's return flight home tomorrow. Probably delayed. Thomas, like all pilots, has a lot of delayed flights. It comes with the territory.

Thomas and I haven't known each other all that long all in all. We'd worked together a short time on the annual staff in college, but he'd been a senior and I'd been a sophomore. Four years after he'd graduated and moved on, he'd walked into my art gallery. That was about a year ago.

Although he'd remembered me, I hadn't recognized him right away.

Six months later we were married.

Thomas always seemed to be in a hurry to do things. He'd been in a hurry to get married. In a hurry to buy a house. He just didn't have much sense of delayed gratification. I'd teased him about it, finding it a bit endearing.

And he was charming enough that he was able to convince me to go along with most things. With me being one of the least impulsive people I knew, he amused me. I rather liked that he pulled me out of my comfort zone on occasion.

I exit off the freeway and head toward my gated neighborhood.

Katy, oddly enough, typically has more traffic than downtown, but this time of night, the roads are pretty much empty.

I drive through the gate, make the five turns required to

get to my house, then pull into the garage. Turn off the motor and open my door to the welcome quiet.

The storm still rages outside, but inside the garage, it's blissfully quiet.

It's usually not so bad going from one garage to the next. Even when it's brutally hot outside. Work to home. The rain, however, makes the drive tricky and tonight was one of the worst storms I've driven through.

But I made it.

I let myself inside and head straight upstairs to the bedroom to change clothes.

Just as I step out of my heels, my phone rings again. I pull it out of my purse and glare at the number.

It's the same number. John from the FAA.

"Hello John," I say. "Do you have my husband's phone number?"

"Yes," he says. "But it's you I need to talk to."

I sit down hard on the little bench in my closet as realization slams into me. Glancing over at Thomas's clothes, neatly hung and organized, I smell his cologne from where he'd gotten dressed earlier in the day.

Thomas always calls when he lands. I'd gotten so busy with the gallery event and then driving in the storm, I only now realized that I hadn't heard from him.

I glance at the time. He should have landed about three hours ago. Three hours.

I'd been so distracted, it hadn't even occurred to me until this minute that he hadn't checked in.

"Why? Has something happened?" I ask, remembering

that I'm on the phone with John with the FAA. "He should be in Austin." I have an overwhelming urge to hang up and dial Thomas's phone number. "The storm..."

"Yes. The storm that's over Houston now came down from the west."

"So Thomas got delayed." That would explain things. He got delayed and he didn't call because he knew I had an important event tonight. But that didn't explain why John from the FAA was on the phone with me.

"He didn't get delayed."

I thought for a minute. Thomas had taken me flying plenty of times. He'd taught me some basics. Flight plans. Weather reports. He was careful.

"A detour then. They had to detour him to another airport." Despite my optimist words, there's a knot forming in the pit of my stomach.

"He radioed in with engine trouble."

"Engine trouble? Emergency landing then." Panic is in my voice now replacing the annoyance. My phone is on speaker, but I'm surprised the phone itself doesn't crack with my herculean grip.

"Audrey. We lost contact with your husband's plane about five pm."

Just Breathe

PREVIEW

Chapter 2
Audrey

Two mornings later, I wander downstairs, wearing sweatpants and a t-shirt, my hair pulled back in a messy ponytail, where my two sisters are in the kitchen.

"Who are these people?" I ask, mostly to myself. I don't expect an answer.

There are people in my house. I don't like people in my house.

I didn't invite them.

Neighbors from the looks of them.

People I've never even met.

Sitting on my sofa. Talking in hushed tones. Light chuckles. Furtive glances in my direction.

We stand behind the island looking out over toward my living room.

Lilah, the youngest, is cutting an apple pie into slices and placing them on plates. Not saying much of anything.

Brianna, a year younger than me, stands next to me, hands on her hips.

"That's Mark and Mary sitting together on the sofa. They live two houses down on the corner. Melissa is sitting on the hearth in front of the fireplace. Her husband Kevin is standing next to her. They live next to you on the other side. And the guy standing at the patio door looking out is Bert. He's the president of your Home Owner's Association."

I look at Brianna, my mouth open in awe. "How do you know this? Never mind." Brianna talks to everybody. She never meets a stranger. But even more important. "How do they even know about Thomas?"

"It was on the news," Lilah says, washing the knife.

"It was on the news?" I ask Brianna.

Their gazes land on me at once—startled, uncertain, as if I've just confessed something unthinkable.

"It's okay," Brianna says, pulling me into a hug. "You're okay."

Lilah puts the knife away and arranges the saucers of pie slices on a tray.

I groan when the doorbell rings. "Why so many people?"

"I'll get it," Brianna says. "Lilah. Give Audrey some pie."

"I'm not hungry," I say, but I sit down at the breakfast table, and take the fork Lilah hands me.

I'm still feeling groggy. Someone, Brianna I think, gave me something to help me sleep last night. I'd slept for... I glance at my watch... twelve hours. I never sleep that long.

After distributing the pie to my guests, which makes absolutely no sense to me, Lilah sits down next to me with her own piece of pie.

"It's good, huh?" Lilah asks as she takes a bite. Lilah never eats sweets. Things must be really bad for Lilah to eat pie.

"Yes." Surprisingly so. "Who made it?"

"HEB I think. I don't know who brought it."

Brianna comes back from answering the front door with a man wearing a suit in tow.

I glance at him out of the corner of my eye, then take another bite of pie. I have a good case of not caring. Learning that one's husband was killed in an airplane crash will do that to a person.

"This is Andrew Harrington," Brianna says, then lowers her voice. "Your attorney."

Alarmed, I look up at Andrew Harrington. "I have an attorney?"

He holds out a hand. "I'm Andrew," he says, kindly.

I set my fork down and put my hand in his.

"Is there someplace we can talk?" he asks. "In private."

"Lilah, get Mr. Harrington some pie, would you?" She turns back to Andrew. "Give me ten minutes and I'll have everyone out of here."

Andrew sits down across from me and dutifully eats the slice of pie Lilah puts in front of him.

Brianna takes the empty tray back into the living room.

"Thank y'all so much for coming," she says in what I recognize as her sweetest voice. "But we're gonna need a bit of privacy now."

Five minutes later she has my five unwanted guests herded out the door.

"We can talk now," she tells Andrew as she sits down at the table.

With Lilah on one side of me and Brianna on the other, I brace myself to hear what the attorney I didn't know I had has to say.

Just Breathe

PREVIEW

Chapter 3
Madison

"I've gone over all the paperwork," Andrew Harrington, Attorney says, taking a pair of wire-rimmed glasses out of his pocket and putting them on.

With the pie cleared away, I sit with my hands in my lap, watching him with heavy eyes.

He seems like a kind man. He has kind eyes and his tone is soft and understanding. Even so, it doesn't do much to keep the lump in my throat at bay.

The single word *widow* keeps swirling through my head. I'm too young to be a widow.

"I'm sorry," Brianna says glancing over at me. "Would you repeat that?"

"Sorry," I say, under my breath. My sister somehow knew my attention had wandered.

"Sure," Andrew says, looking into my eyes.

"Thomas made me executor of your estate, so I consulted with your accountant. I can skip over some of the details for now, but let me just boil it down.

"I'm afraid you're going to have to sell the house."

I blink at him. "Okay." Last night when the thought of living out here in Katy by myself crossed my mind, I'd shut it down. It wasn't something I could wrap my head around. But here he was bringing it up.

"You're okay with that?" Andrew asks.

"She needs to think about it," Brianna says.

"No," I say. "I don't need to think about it. I'm okay with it."

"Good," Andrew says. "That's good."

"So she'll have money, right?" Brianna asks. "From the sale of the house and insurance. She'll have insurance to start over, right?"

Frowning, Andrew rubs a hand over his face and removes his reading glasses.

"I regret to tell you the insurance is already allocated," he says.

"Already allocated?" Brianna says. "For what?"

"Thomas had some debt. Some rather large debts and even larger obligations."

Brianna looks at me. "What kind of debts did Thomas

have?"

"I don't know. I didn't know he had any debts." I look outside at the mimosa tree Thomas had planted. He'd been so proud of himself when he'd dug that hole all by himself and dropped the five-foot tall tree we'd hauled from Home Depot into it.

"What kind of debts?" I ask Andrew.

"He had some pretty significant credit card debt, another mortgage, and—"

"Wait." Brianna holds up a hand. "Another mortgage?"

Andrew glances at me. Sits up a little straighter. "He has a condo in downtown Houston."

"Since when?" I ask. Thomas had never told me about him having another condo. When we'd met, he'd lived in an apartment near the Galleria.

"We can come back to those details."

"No. The condo is a mistake. There's no condo." I feel a little dizzy. A little faint. If there was a condo, I should know about it.

"Five years. It's not a mistake."

I steel myself for the sudden realization that I hardly knew Thomas at all. "Tell me why. Why did Thomas have a condo he never told me about?"

Neither one of my sisters says anything as I wait for Andrew to tell us these things about my husband. Things I hadn't known. Things I should have known.

"The child," Andrew says. "Thomas has a child."

I squeeze my eyes closed and Brianna grips my hand.

Lilah watches us all closely, then turns on Andrew. "You

came all the way out here just to tell her this?" I hear the anger in Lilah's voice.

"It's okay, Lilah," I say, looking at her.

"No. It's not okay." She pins her gaze on Andrew. "If you don't have something good to tell Audrey, you can go. Can't you see she's already devastated?"

"I'm so sorry," Andrew says. "But I do have good news."

All three of us just look at him. A gust of warm Texas wind flutters a branch of the mimosa tree against the window.

"His grandfather left him a cabin. It's just outside a small town in the Colorado mountains."

"Who does that go to?" Brianna asks with obvious ire in her tone.

"It's protected. According to the grandfather's will, in the event that something happens to Thomas, it specifically goes to Thomas's first wife."

"Am I his first wife?" I ask, my voice sounding small. I no longer trust anything I thought I knew about my marriage.

Thomas has a child. A child with someone else. He'd never told me about having a child.

"Yes," Andrew says. "You're his first wife."

"The cabin is free and clear of any debts." He clears his throat. "There's a stipend that comes with it."

"So I own a house in Colorado?"

"Yes. Sort of. It's in a trust. It's yours but you have to live in it. You have to live in the house for one year for it to be yours. As long as you live there, you get the stipend that comes with it. But you can never sell the house."

"Thomas said we'd go to Colorado one day. I thought he meant we'd go there for a vacation."

"Audrey can't just move off to Colorado," Brianna says. "She has a job here. A life. Family."

"The cabin is paid for?" Lilah asks.

"Free and clear. All expenses paid by an executor."

"It must be a dump," Brianna says. "She can't live in a dump."

"It's not a dump," Andrew says.

"You've seen it?" Lilah asks, pinning Andrew with her gaze.

"No. But I've seen photos."

"Who's the executor?" I ask.

"I am," Andrew says.

Brianna sits back and crosses her arms. "It sounds fishy to me."

"What town?" I ask. "What town in Colorado?"

"Whiskey Springs."

Whiskey Springs. I'll think about it. Maybe something will come to me. A conversation. A mention.

But I know it won't. Just like the child. Apparently Andrew was a vault when it came to his personal life.

"How much is the stipend?" Lilah asks.

"The stipend is one million dollars."

"In lieu of millions of dollars in insurance," Brianna says, through gritted teeth. "The wife gets stuck with a cabin in the middle of nowhere and a million dollars. It won't last anytime." She looks at me. "You should contest the will."

"He has a child," I say. I don't even know who's side I'm

on at this point. I'm just numb. Trying to hold all this information in my groggy brain and process it.

"So? He should have told you."

"And he shouldn't have died," I say. What I don't say is I shouldn't be a widow. I should not be a widow at twenty-seven.

"Ladies," Andrew says. "I'm going to leave some papers for you to look over. I'd like to come back in a couple of days after you've had some time to absorb everything."

My sisters glare at him.

"Okay," I say. "I need time to think about everything. And right now I'm very tired."

"I understand. I hate to be the one to drop all this on you. But..." He pulls a stack of papers from the briefcase at his feet. "There's one thing I think I need to clarify."

"Okay."

"The stipend. There's enough money in the account to last all of your lifetimes put together and it's in an account that compounds daily." He leans forward, his gaze locked on mine. "The stipend will be deposited in your account the day you sign the papers. One million dollars. Every year. In perpetuity."

Just Breathe

PREVIEW

Chapter 4
Audrey

"She can't go," Brianna says.

"She can't not go," Lilah says.

The three of us sit in my living room on the big sectional with nothing but the flames from the fireplace for light. The contract papers are scattered in front of us on the coffee table. Already dog-eared and highlighted.

It's dark now. After Andrew had left, I'd gone upstairs to take a nap. It seems like I can't get enough sleep.

Without reading it, I left the paperwork with my sisters

to examine. And they had. I'll read it all later. Tomorrow maybe.

They'd gone through everything line by line. Brianna worked for an attorney for a year so she'd felt qualified to go through the paperwork line by line. Then she and Lilah had discussed it while I slept.

They'd even sent it over to our Uncle Carl. Uncle Carl is an attorney.

After I'd gotten up, they'd had pizza delivered of which I'd eaten all of one slice.

Not content with me eating just one slice of pizza, Lilah had made popcorn and set it out. I grab a handful and nibble on it.

"Audrey doesn't know anything about the mountains."

"How much different can it be than Katy?" Lilah, obviously not a fan of Katy, wrinkles her nose and picks up a bowl of popcorn. She doesn't eat sweets, but she'll eat anything salty. All ninety-five pounds of her.

"Have you ever been in the mountains?"

"She'll be fine. It's not just a cabin. It's a big house and it has maid service."

"I don't trust it." Brianna sits back and crosses her arms.

"You do know I'm right here," I say.

They both turn and look at me. I honestly think they had forgotten I was sitting right here.

"Of course we do," Brianna says.

"Is that in the contract?" I ask. "The maid service?"

"Yes," Lilah says, her face brightening. "We pulled up pictures on the Internet. Do you want to see them?"

"Sure." I shrug. I'm curious. For a lot of reasons. Not the least of which is why Lilah is suddenly fighting against Brianna for me to go to the cabin.

She links her phone to the big screen television—one of Thomas's prized possessions—on the wall over the fireplace and pulls up Google Earth. Types in the address.

"I see a lot of trees." Squinting, I lean forward. "And a rooftop. I can't tell anything about it."

"See," Brianna says. "It's blocked or something."

"It might be blocked," I say, munching on popcorn. "Some private residences are."

"You're both missing the point," Lilah says. "It's big. It's not just a cabin."

"Andrew said he has pictures. Did you ask him to send them over?"

They both look blankly at me. Then they look at each other.

I locate his business card on the coffee table and send him a text asking for pictures.

"Now," I say. "We just wait. He'll send..."

My phone vibrates.

"He must have been waiting."

"You have photos?" Lilah asks. "Put them up on the television."

I have three photographs. The first one is of the outside of the house.

"It looks like a lodge," Brianna says. "Two stories."

"Three if you count the attic." Lilac stands up to move

closer to the television. "Look how pretty it is. It looks a log cabin but with glass. Look at all the windows. "

"We don't know how old the photos are," Brianna says.

Lilah turns on her. "Since when did you become so negative?"

"Since my sister is thinking about moving to the other side of the world to live."

"It's not the other side of the world," I say, keeping my eyes on the photo. Taking in the what is supposed to be a cabin, but looks more like a lodge just as Brianna pointed out.

"Couldn't be much worse than Katy," Lilah grumbles.

I don't say anything, but I tend to agree with Lilah. Something about the place looks so peaceful.

"Thomas never said anything to you about it?" Lilah asks.

I shake my head and lower my gaze to my phone.

"Lilah," Brianna admonishes.

"It's okay. We have to talk about him eventually." I slide to the next photo.

The inside of the cabin looks surprisingly modern with lots of light. An open floorplan much like this house.

"Look at that view," Lilah says. "You can sit in your living room and look out at the mountains."

"If she goes," Brianna says.

"I wonder if it's furnished," I say.

"It is. Fully furnished."

"That might not be the same furniture it has now."

"Brianna. Stop it."

"It doesn't matter," I say. "I don't need a lot. And with the stipend if I don't like it, I can replace it." I slide to the next photo.

"Look at that fireplace," Lilah says. "I think that's real wood."

Brianna bites her tongue.

"I can learn how to light a real fire," I say, knowing what Brianna is thinking. "How hard can it be?"

No one says anything for long enough that I shift my gaze to Lilah, then Brianna.

"You lost," Lilah says to Brianna.

"I know."

"Lost what?"

"The bet. I bet that you would be. Brianna bet that you wouldn't. I won."

"I haven't decided yet."

"You can't not go," Lilah says.

"She can live with me," Brianna offers.

"In your one-bedroom apartment? No thank you."

"Our parents."

I'm already shaking my head. "I'm definitely not moving back to Atlanta."

"By the way," Brianna says. "Our parents will be here in the morning."

"They should have just driven," Lilah says. "They'd be here by now."

"It's too hard on them. They're too old."

"They didn't have to come," I say. But I knew they'd be here for the funeral.

"It'll be good," Brianna says. "They can help pack."

"So they're too old to drive, but not too old to help pack?"

Brianna shrugs.

"Again. No need. I'm going to pack up my personal things and let the rest go with the house." I look up at the photo on the television. "It looks like my next place has everything I need."

Lilah is right.

I'm going.

Moving to Katy hadn't been my idea, but I'd gone along with it.

And Thomas had left everything to a child I hadn't even known he had.

And he might not even have known about it or intended it, but he'd left me a cabin in the mountains. Along with a healthy stipend.

I'm not going to let this opportunity slip by me.

Keep Reading Just Breathe...

Secrets and Second Chances

Honeymoon with a Stranger

Not Our Wedding

(SILVER PINES)

The Way Back to You

Back to Where We Began

When We Were Us

(ONCE UPON FOREVER)

My Forever Guy

Our Forever Love

Forever Vows

Finding Forever

Accidentally Forever

(TRUE NORTH)

Borrowed Until Monday

Still Mine

The Moon and the Stars at Christmas

Perfectly Mismatched

On the Way to Forever

A Merry Little Christmas

On the Way Home to Christmas

It was Always You

(UNBREAK MY HEART)

Begin Again

Love Again

Falling Again

(FOR THE LOVE OF THE FLIGHT)

Just Stay

Just Chance

Just Believe

Just Us

Just Once

Just Happened

Just Maybe

Just Pretend

Just Because

(MAGNETIC NORTH)

Second Chance Kisses

Second Chance Secrets

First Time Charm

Three Broken Rules

Second Chance Destiny

Unexpected Vows

(FALLING FOR CHRISTMAS)

The Heart of Christmas

The Magic of Christmas

In a One Horse Open Sleigh

A Secret Royal Christmas

An Old Fashioned Christmas

(CITY SKYLINE BILLIONAIRES)

Billionaire's Unexpected Landing

Billionaire's Accidental Girlfriend

Billionaire's Fallen Angel

Billionaire's Secret Crush

Billionaire's Barefoot Bride

(TRULY, MADLY, DEEPLY)

The Lady in the Red Dress

On the Edge of Chance

Sealed with a Kiss

Kiss Me at Midnight

The Heart Knows

(STOLEN ECHOES)

When Cupid's Arrow Strikes

Chasing Fireflies

A Chance Encounter

(EDGE OF THE HORIZON)

The Forever Equation

Pretend Boyfriend

All our Tomorrows

Kissing for Keeps

Out of the Blue

The Princess and the Playboy

(RED LIPSTICK KISSES)

Red Lipstick Kisses and Small Town Wishes

Stolen Dances and Big City Chances

Chance Connections and Upside Down Plans

A Christmas Kiss on the Twenty-Fifth

Believe in the Magic of Christmas

Vows of Inheritance Series
(Reading Order)

Vow to Protect

Vow to Redeem

ROMANTASY

(IN THE SPIRIT OF LOVE)

Spirits of the Heart

Out of Dreams and Ashes

Etched Upon the Heart

WESTERN ROMANCE

(LONE STAR HEARTS)

Wanted by a Texas Ranger

Saved by a Texas Ranger

(WHISKEY SPRINGS)

Finding Natalie

Promising Samantha

Falling for Allyson

Saving Savannah

Claiming Charlie

Rescuing Keira

Protecting Gabriella

Courting Isabella

TIME TRAVEL

(INTO THE MIST)

Written in the Wind

Scripted in the Stars

Destined in the Twilight

Promised in the Mist

Trapped in the Melody

(DRAGON'S BLOOD)

Dragon's Blood

Lavender Blue

Champagne Silver

Twilight Frost

Mountbatten Pink

(WHEN HEARTSTRINGS BECKON)

Rescued in Time

Meet me in 1879

(WHEN HEARTSTRINGS ECHO)

Messages Across Time

Falling Through to Forever

Once Upon a Winter's Spell

(BECKONED)

Before the Storm

Twist of Fate

When the Stars Align

Once Upon a Christmas

Once in a Blue Moon

A Wish Upon a Star

(BEGUILED)

When Lightning Strikes

Storm of Time

Midnight Storm

When the Moon Falls

Stormborn Angel

(SPELLED)

Time Tempest

The Heart Remembers

A Moment in Time

Moonlight Shadows

HISTORICAL

(TAPESTRY OF BLUE AND GRAY)

Shadows Beneath Magnolia Blooms

Secrets Among Southern Roses

(IT HAPPENED BY ACCIDENT)

Accidentally Alluring

Accidentally Married

(SOUTHERN BELLE CIVIL WAR)

Beyond Enemy Lines

Love Always

Hearts Under Siege

Hearts Under Fire

Away Down South in Dixie

The Reluctant Bride

Stay with Me

Jasmine Kisses

Magnolia Kisses

Gardenia Kisses

(THE QUINNS)

Wait for Me

Take Me Home

Keep Me Safe

FATED MATES

Riley's Mate

Aiden's Mate

Brayden's Mate

STANDALONE SUSPENSE

Lost and Found

All I Want for Christmas

Serenity

Courting Alley Cat

All of the books in each Series are standalone and can be read out of order. However, some books have characters from the previous stories in them.

Sign up for my NEWSLETTER to get all my romance releases, sales, Kickstarter announcements, and a **FREE** romance, SEALED WITH A KISS